"No, Roger, it's okay. I can do it," Chrissy said, trying to wrestle the mop from him.

"Oh, but I insist—it will go much more quickly with two." He tugged at the mop once more and Chrissy gave up the struggle at the same moment.

"Okay, take it," she said, then watched as Roger went flying backward with the mop, staggered to regain his balance, then put his foot into the bucket.

"Roger, watch out!" Chrissy yelled too late as the dogs began barking again.

Roger shook his foot. "Now there's a pail on my foot!" he said with a sigh. "How to impress a girl. First give her heart failure, then kick over a bucket and get it stuck on your foot. Nice going, Roger!"

He looked so funny, staring down with such big eyes at his bucket-encased foot. Chrissy tried not to giggle but couldn't help it.

"Do you think you could help me get this thing off?" he asked politely. "I'm really not enjoying this much, and I don't want to walk home three blocks with a bucket on my foot, so please help pull it off."

He gave Chrissy such a hopeful smile that she stopped laughing and smiled back.

Other books in the **SUGAR & SPICE** series:

COMING SOON:

Janet Quin-Harkin's

Sugar & Spice

Flip Side

IVY BOOKS • NEW YORK

Ivy Books
Published by Ballantine Books
Copyright © 1987 by Butterfield Press, Inc. & Janet Quin-Harkin

Produced by Butterfield Press, Inc.
133 Fifth Avenue
New York, New York 10003

Library of Congress Catalog Card Number: 87-90914

ISBN 0-8041-0051-9

Manufactured in the United States of America

First Edition: October 1987

FLIP SIDE

Janet Quin-Harkin

Chapter 1

"Rats, double rats, and triple rats!" Chrissy Madden yelled as she slammed the front door behind her and stomped along the hallway to her bedroom.

As she stormed into the room, she noticed her cousin Caroline looking at her curiously from the chair by the window.

"What?" Caroline asked. "Have you been out collecting rodents, or is that an old Iowa spell?"

Chrissy simply glared at her cousin. This wasn't a time to joke around. "Very funny," she growled, throwing her bookbag down in the corner so that the ornaments on her chest of drawers trembled.

"Do I get just the slightest hint that you are displeased with something?" Caroline asked evenly, peering over the pages of her French

1

textbook. "I don't know what gave me that idea, but I'm very sensitive about picking up bad vibes!"

Chrissy grinned sheepishly and sank to her bed across the room from Caroline. "I've just come from the bank," she said. "And I find that I have a grand total of three dollars and thirty-five cents in my account."

"Well, Chrissy, we've just been on a trip," Caroline reminded her. "You bought lots of lovely presents for your folks back home and new clothes for the trip. Money can't last forever!"

"I know," Chrissy said with a big sigh. "My dad asked me just before we left if I was okay for money, and I told him I was fine, because I know how tight money has been on the farm recently. I really thought I was fairly fine, too—at least fifty dollars or so—but three dollars, Cara, I still can't understand where it all went."

"It went on gracious living, Chrissy," Caroline said with a smile. "Besides spending money on the trip to Iowa, you've gotten used to movies and pizzas and ice-cream sundaes and things since you came to stay with us in San Francisco. And new clothes, too—you must have bought yourself a whole new wardrobe."

"I guess I have spent a lot," Chrissy admitted. She kicked off her sneakers, which landed with a thud on the floor. "That money was supposed to last me all school year. But I still have two more months of school to go, and then I wanted to travel around a bit before I go back to good old Danbury, Iowa."

"Somehow I don't think three dollars is going to take you very far," Caroline remarked dryly.

"No kidding! Three dollars won't even buy me two slices of pepperoni pizza and a large Coke." Chrissy gave another big sigh. "It's just not fair, Cara. I came back from our spring vacation in Iowa all excited and full of energy and ready to make the most of my last weeks in the city. I was planning to go to every theater I'd missed so far and Giants baseball games and beaches and museums and try Vietnamese and Indonesian food and eat a whole 'Earthquake' at the ice-cream parlor." She flopped back onto her pillow. "All my dreams crushed by a blow of fate! My last chance to be a swinging city slicker snuffed out!"

Caroline smiled and shook her head at Chrissy's dramatic expression. "Cheer up," she said. "We can't have two of us depressed at the same time."

Chrissy opened her eyes and focused sharply on Caroline. She should have realized that her cousin had been even quieter than usual lately. "You're still feeling pretty low?" she asked softly.

Caroline nodded and turned her head away, but not before Chrissy caught a glimpse of a tear sliding down her cheek. "I'm trying to get over Luke, but I still miss him dreadfully, Chrissy," Caroline said at last. "Who would ever have thought that I'd fall in love with the most unlikely boy in the world? It was just plain stupid of me, wasn't it? I mean, we both knew nothing could ever come of it. He's a farm boy who is only happy in the wide-open spaces, and I'm a city girl who prefers busy streets with a deli on every corner. I'm trying so hard to get over him, but I just can't." Her voice cracked as she spoke, and Chrissy felt immediately guilty that she had been making her usual dramatic fuss about something that really wasn't important when Caroline was still crying inside. She got up and walked across to her cousin, putting her hand gently on Caroline's shoulder.

"These things take time, Cara," she said. "You can't just switch off loving somebody because you tell yourself to. And who knows—things change, people change. Either you'll meet somebody else who is just as special, or you'll find a way to be together. I'm a great believer in fate, Cara. After all, I've been very philosophical about Ben, haven't I?"

"You certainly have," Caroline agreed. "I'm amazed at the cool way you handled that. It can't have been easy for you to find that you no longer have enough in common with your boyfriend to keep up a relationship after three years. He's such a nice guy, too. . . ."

Chrissy looked down at the floor where a big triangle of sunlight was turning the beige carpet into a rich honey color. "I know that," she said quietly, "and believe me, there are still times when I ask myself if I've been completely crazy to give him up. I wake up sometimes at night and

I miss him so much it hurts, but I know it couldn't work anymore. He still thinks like a farm boy, Cara. All we'd do is give each other heartaches." She looked back at Caroline and managed a little smile. "I've had a taste of city life now. I won't be treated like the little lady who stays home to cook and clean anymore."

Chrissy was glad to see she had cheered up her cousin—at least for the moment.

"Chrissy, I don't remember you ever being a little lady who cooked and cleaned," Caroline said, laughing. "Your brownies are like rocks, and as for cleaning—well, just look at your side of the room!"

Chrissy put on her best "We are not amused" look. "I always knew I was destined for bigger and better things than home ec," she said. "That's why I'm looking forward to this last quarter of school here. I'm signing up for ceramics and marine biology as electives. They are two things I'd never get to do back home."

"Especially the marine biology," Caroline said, curling her legs around her again like a cat in her chair. "The course would be somewhat expensive if they had to fly you a thousand miles for each tidepool."

Chrissy grinned broadly. "So many exciting things are happening in school right now," she said. Then she grew sad again. Chrissy's whole face seemed to glow when she was excited, so that when the excitement left her face it was like turning off a light. "I wanted to get involved in so many things—there's a weekend at Yosemite National Park, and marine biology is going down to the Monterey Aquarium, and there are two theater evenings coming up. I wanted to do them all. I want to see everything and do everything in California before I go home, and I figured they'd help me stop thinking about Ben and whether I was crazy. But there's a slight problem . . . everything costs money! that's why I popped into the bank just now. I wanted to see how many outings I could afford. It was an awful shock when that snooty woman handed me my little book with the three dollars printed out in it. She was horrible, Cara."

"What do you mean?" Caroline asked. "It's not the bank teller's fault that you only have three dollars."

"I know that," Chrissy replied. "It's just that I thought there had to be some mistake, so I asked her in my nicest voice to check again, but she got mad. So I got mad back."

"What did you say, Chrissy?"

"I just said that maybe she was missing a zero or two on her calculations, and if she didn't check my balance again, I'd go behind the counter and do it myself. Then before I knew it, two security officers came running up with their guns drawn."

Caroline shook her head, laughing. "*Mama mìa*, Chrissy, you do get yourself in trouble," she said. "You should write a book on your life here when you get home. Call it *Three Hundred Ways to Get in Trouble in San Francisco!*"

"Very funny. Ha, ha!" Chrissy said. "You're my cousin. You are supposed to be sympathetic, not laugh. It wasn't funny at all, believe me, when those two guards pointed guns in my direction."

"No, I'm sure it wasn't," Caroline said, managing to sober up. "I'm sorry, Chrissy. It hasn't been a good day for you, has it?"

"Not by a long shot," Chrissy admitted. "I got an F on my math test, too."

"In which case, I'll let you join me in depression," Caroline said.

"But I don't even have enough money for a Cable car special at Mama's Ice Cream Parlor," Chrissy said. "Boy, that always relieves my depression."

"I haven't gone to Mama's since I broke up with Alex," Caroline commented thoughtfully. "That ice-cream parlor always reminded me too painfully of him. But now I might just try it again—if I can come up with the money myself, that is. At least one good thing came out of my heartbreak over Luke—I'm not pining for Alex anymore!"

"Isn't it a weird world," Chrissy said, a thoughtful expression on her face. "I wonder how many boys we will fall in and out of love with before we finally meet the right man for us?"

"I hope not too many more," Caroline commented. "I feel like I'm being torn apart every time."

"What you need is something to take your mind off Luke," Chrissy said, starting to pace up and down the room. "Are there any good after-school activities this quarter that you're thinking of going out for?"

Caroline rolled her eyes upward. "Did you look at the bulletin board?" she asked. "Track or softball and a debating contest. None of those is really me, I'm afraid. I wish I could get an after-school job, but with my amount of homework, I don't see how I could juggle it."

Chrissy's eyes lit up. "After-school job?" she asked. "What a great idea! I'd almost forgotten we'd turned sixteen now. People will hire us. I could earn enough money to do all the things I want. . . ." She started to jump up and down excitedly, so that the floor shook and the crabby old woman in the apartment downstairs began thumping on her ceiling. "Cara, you are a genius! You've solved all my problems. I'll get a job, I'll buy clothes, I'll travel . . . What about a car, too? I could drive around California in my own car!"

Caroline started laughing. "Chrissy—minimum wage is not going to provide you with a car in two months," she said.

"Minimum wage?" Chrissy asked in horror. "If I get a job, I'm going for the best."

Caroline went on laughing. "Somehow I don't think the Bank of America is holding open a vice-president's job for you," she said. "Kids' jobs always pay badly. You'll probably have to start with fast food."

Chrissy's eyes lit up again. "Well, that wouldn't be so bad, would it? If they let you eat all the hamburgers and fries you want while you're on duty..."

"Kids at school who've tried it don't think it's too wonderful," Caroline said soberly. "Why don't we take the want ads to school tomorrow and ask our friends if they have any bright ideas? Maybe I can find a job, too—one that would fit in with my schedule. I could sure use some spending money...."

Chrissy danced over to Caroline. "Hey, wouldn't it be great if we got a job together? We could be career women tearing through rush hour in our dark suits and sneakers. We'd look so important with briefcases and everything!"

Caroline started to laugh again. "You are a dope," she said. "All I can visualize us doing together is putting two all-beef patties between sesame seed buns."

"That's your trouble," Chrissy said proudly. "You don't think big. I am now going to make myself a hearty snack to prepare my body for tomorrow's job search...." She started to walk toward the door, chin held high as she had watched important career women in the city walk. She reached the door, and suddenly her excitement overpowered her sophisticated image. "Ya*hoo!*" she yelled. "We're going to be rich! We're going to be rich!" And she sprinted down the hall with such energy that old Mrs. Langdon downstairs started thumping with her cane again.

Chapter 2

"Now this is what I call spring weather," Justine said, lying back on the soft green grass of the little park and closing her eyes.

Caroline and Chrissy's friends usually met in this small pocket of green between apartment blocks whenever the weather was right, which in San Francisco usually meant the fall and spring and very seldom the summer.

"Make the most of it," Randy, Justine's boyfriend, commented dryly. "If it keeps up much longer, the fog will be rolling in and we'll be shivering up here again."

Justine opened her ice-blue eyes and looked at him coldly. "Did anyone ever mention to you that you are a pessimist?" she asked.

"Frequently," Randy said with a big smile. "My

mother says I was such a depressing baby that she almost left me on a church doorstep."

The rest of the group giggled. Justine propped herself up on her elbow and looked at him tenderly. "I don't know why I put up with you," she said.

"It must be my great body," Randy replied, lying back with a contented sigh beside her and then grunting in alarm as she hit him with the French book she was studying.

"I think there should be a law that says students do not have to attend afternoon classes on sunny days," Tracy said firmly. "I always get so relaxed and drowsy up here at the park that I fall asleep in afternoon classes. It's so embarrassing if the teacher catches your head nodding."

"I know," agreed Maria. "In American history I sit by a window, and you know how boring old Todd is—one day I really nodded off, and my head went clunk against the glass. Now *that* was embarrassing."

"You should have seen Harvey Holloman back home." Chrissy looked up from feeding a hopeful circle of sparrows. "Now he was a guy who could really sleep in class. One day our eighth-grade teacher decided to teach him a lesson—he had two boys carry him out, chair and all, and put him in the snow in the middle of the football field."

"Oh, come on, Chrissy," Tracy said, laughing. "You're kidding us."

"No, really," Chrissy said. "It actually happened, you can ask anyone in Danbury."

"So what happened when they put him down in the snow?" asked Tracy.

Chrissy grinned. "Even then he didn't wake up—but then the poor guy was up for milking at four every morning, so I guess he had a right to be tired by the afternoon."

"What are you reading, Cara?" Justine asked suspiciously. "Don't tell me you're still studying for the French test. You know you'll get an A anyway. It is sickening the way you get A's in French."

Caroline looked up at Justine and smiled. "I wasn't studying, actually," she said. "I was reading the want ads. Chrissy and I are looking for jobs. We're both very short of cash after our little trip to Iowa."

"I think that people who go on trips in the middle of the school year and are allowed to miss a whole week of school deserve to suffer," Randy said severely. "While we were slaving over horrible math tests and English essays, you two were basking in the sun in Iowa."

Caroline and Chrissy looked at each other and laughed. "Hardly," Chrissy said. "There was a blizzard while we were there. Caroline had gone flying in a small plane and got caught in the snow."

"Oh, really?" The others looked up with interest. Chrissy realized that she shouldn't have opened her mouth, but it was too late.

"You didn't tell us about that, Cara—the most

exciting part of your trip, too. What happened?"
Justine asked.

"Nothing much," Caroline said, her cheeks
bright pink. "We had to land in a field and take
shelter in an old house."

"Sounds pretty exciting to me," said Maria.
"Weren't you scared?"

"I was for a while," Caroline admitted, "but it
was okay once we found shelter."

"Now if that had happened to me, I'd have
relived it in gory detail for everyone I met,"
Randy said. "The swirling snow, the long slow
crawl toward the house . . . am I going to make
it? Is that frostbite on my fingers?"

Justine gave him a playful push. "Yes, well, we
all know you, Randy. You can dramatize having a
splinter taken from your finger!"

Chrissy glanced across at Caroline. She knew
very well why her cousin did not want to talk
about the blizzard. It was during that blizzard
that she and Luke had fallen in love while
stranded in an old deserted farmhouse. Chrissy
could just imagine how romantic that must have
been, but she knew that Caroline wouldn't want
to talk about it now.

"So getting back to jobs," she said brightly,
changing the subject. "Who's got a brilliant idea
for us to earn lots of money?"

"I wish I knew," Tracy said. "I'd be doing it, too."

"Don't look at me," Maria said with a big sigh.
"I have to work for my parents at the bakery

whenever I have free time, and I'm lucky if I get paid a dime."

"What would you like to do, if you could have any job you wanted?" Randy asked, moving next to Caroline so he could study the want ads.

Chrissy shrugged. "Easy, interesting work that makes lots of money," she said. "I really don't know, Randy. The only paid work I've ever done is helping tag the hogs on the next-door farm and give them their shots."

The others burst out laughing. Chrissy laughed along with them, even though she always felt uncomfortable when kids here laughed like that. She never knew whether they were laughing with her or at her.

"That should be a very useful skill on job applications," Randy quipped. " 'Tell me, Miss Madden, why do you think you are equipped to work at Neiman-Marcus?' 'Well, I have had experience tagging hogs.' 'Oh, very good, just what we need. You can start by piercing ears at our jewelry counter!' "

More laughter.

"What sort of job are you thinking of, Cara?" Randy cut in. "Is there anything in the paper?"

Caroline looked up with a sigh. "Nothing, as usual—unless you are over eighteen and have tons of experience. Anyway, I don't really know if I can handle a job. I want one, and heaven knows I need the money, but with my homework schedule, I don't know what I could do. SATs are coming up soon, don't forget!"

"Caroline is going to show us all up and get a perfect score on all her exams," Justine said. "Then she'll be offered a scholarship to Stanford and end up as a brilliant . . . What is it you want to be brilliant in, Cara?"

Caroline wriggled in embarrassment. "I don't even know what I want to do yet," she said. "Isn't that dumb? I'm at the end of my junior year, and I don't even know what I want to major in in college yet. There's nothing that I can think of that I really want to study and have a career in."

"You are definitely not going back to any sort of ballet or dance, Cara?" asked Tracy. "I know you said you had given it up forever, but I wondered . . ."

Caroline shook her head very firmly. "I have put on my last toe shoe," she said. "You saw what it did to me, Tracy. It made me a nervous wreck, trying to live up to what everyone else expected of me. The only thing I enjoyed was the performing. I hated all these hours of classes."

Chrissy leaned over Caroline's shoulder, studying the want ads.

"Hey!" she yelled, so close to Caroline's ear that Caroline nearly jumped a mile. "You said there weren't any jobs in here. How about this, then? 'Dancers wanted for club. Experience not necessary'?"

"Chrissy!" Caroline said, half in horror, half laughing.

Chrissy looked indignant. "I can dance!" she said. "Remember I had the solo in *Oklahoma!*"

"But, Chrissy," Tracy said softly, "those advertisements are for strip clubs—you know, topless dancers?"

"Mama mìa!" Chrissy said, turning very pink. "Are you sure?"

The girls grinned. "All the ads for dancers in the paper are for that sort of dancer!"

"I'm glad you stopped me before I went to try out," Chrissy said, recovering with a grin. "I would have fallen through the floor if someone had asked me to take off my clothes! But what about this job?" She peered back at the paper again. "'Cosmetic sales. Good income. Small investment.' Wouldn't that be nice, helping people with their makeup?"

"Chrissy!" Caroline said again. "'Small investment' means you have to buy all the cosmetics before you sell them. You'd have to spend a lot of money, and maybe you wouldn't even get it back. Besides, I don't know if my folks would like you going door to door in the city."

"Then what can I do?" Chrissy asked. "I am definitely going to find myself a job. Do you think maybe I'd do better just walking around the neighborhood and looking for Help Wanted signs in windows?"

"I saw a Help Wanted sign at the Magic Flute Music Store," Maria said suddenly.

"I know Mr. Simon, the owner," Caroline said brightly. "He's a friend of my dad's."

"That job would be right up your alley, Cara,"

Justine said encouragingly. "You know all there is to know about music."

Caroline's face was flushed and excited. "If it didn't take up too much time," she said cautiously, "it might be terrific. Maybe I'll go over there after school."

Chrissy glanced across at Caroline, trying to fight back the annoyance and jealousy. She was the one who really wanted the job most, and nobody had any suggestions for her. Caroline wasn't even sure she wanted a job, and it looked like she'd get the first one she went after!

"I can't let you get a job before me," she said lightly to Caroline. "I'm going to have to tramp the streets and not come home until I'm hired!"

"Way to go, Chrissy," Randy said enthusiastically. "We can't wait for you to get a job so that you can treat us all to ice cream!"

"We are looking for jobs to make some money, Randy," Caroline said sweetly, "not to have our friends eat the profits!"

"Thanks a lot, Cara," Randy said, lifting his head just enough to be able to look at her. "Why, I haven't had an ice-cream sundae since . . . how long has it been, Justine?"

"Sunday," Justine said, laughing at him. "You had a sundae on Sunday."

"That long?" asked Randy. "No wonder I'm suffering from withdrawal symptoms."

The others started to join in with teasing Randy. Chrissy looked from one face to the next. *These kids take so much for granted*, she thought. *They think that everyone in the world eats in restaurants several times a week and goes to movies and theaters. They probably don't even understand how important it is for me to earn my own money now . . . with the farm so uncertain I might have to pay my own way through college, and the sooner I get into the habit of a steady job, the better.* A Mercedes pulled to a halt beside the park, and an elegant woman helped two little children from the backseat. Chrissy's thoughts strayed to Ben's old truck. He had done any job anyone would give him to pay to for that truck— helping with the harvest, cleaning out the pigs, anything. He was really proud of the truck, because it was his own. As she thought of Ben, she felt a pang of sadness and guilt. It wasn't his fault that she had changed. She hadn't wanted to change, she had promised him she'd stay the same person no matter what happened to her in the city. But being with people like Justine and Randy and Tracy had changed her, in some ways for the better, because they had opened her eyes to things she had never dreamed of—college and women's rights and the prospect of an exciting career. But in other ways she had changed for the worse because she now liked Caroline's life-style. She liked eating out and buying new clothes to keep up with fashions and seeing movies as soon as they came out.

I've just got to get a job, she thought, staring past the laughing teenagers to the shimmering water of the bay.

Chapter 3

"Dear, darling, Mom;

"Thanks so much for your letter. I miss you, too. It was wonderful to see you all again. I had such a good time. Of course, now i'm back in the hectic California life-style, and as busy as ever..."

Chrissy chewed on the end of her pen and stared across the empty room. From down the hall came the opening music for a *Loveboat* rerun on TV. She looked down at the paper again. "You know what California is like—all parties and activities every evening, so don't worry about me, okay? I don't even have time to brood about me and Ben, believe it or not. He'll always be special, but in a different way now, so I guess that's life and I'm taking it okay."

There was a burst of canned laughter from the

next room. Chrissy got up with a sigh and walked down the hall to turn off the TV. Without the noise the house seemed very empty.

"For once I'm having a quiet evening to myself tonight," she continued to write. "Caroline's parents have gone to yet another concert—I don't know how they can keep on going to concerts and operas all the time and still enjoy it—but then it is Uncle Richard's job to report on them, so I suppose they have to do it.

"Oh, and speaking of jobs, Caroline has gotten herself a job. She's working at a big music store. In fact, she's there right now because they stay open late on Saturday nights. It's her first evening on the job, and I'm dying to find out how it went. It's really the ideal job for her, because she knows so much about music. I mean, in the Kirby family they talk music at the breakfast table."

Chrissy stared out of the window into the black velvet night outside. The air was perfumed with early summer blossoms, and the night was full of exciting sounds of the city. It would have been a great night to be out with friends, but there was the small problem of three dollars not being enough to buy a movie ticket . . . .

Chrissy swallowed the tears that threatened to come now that she was alone with time to think. The emptiness of the apartment kept reminding her too strongly that she was the only one with nothing to do—that she had no job and no boyfriend and no prospect of either, as far as she could see. She'd spent two very depressing and embarrassing evenings trying to find a job. Caroline had found her job at the Magic Flute so easily, that Chrissy was determined to find her own job without any help. She had tramped the streets, asking at any place with a Help Wanted sign in the window, and even some without.

She squirmed again in embarrassment as she recalled what a horrible couple of days it had been. The usher's job at the movie theater had looked so promising until she'd found out that it was a porno theater, and she'd been sure she could serve in a corner grocery until she'd realized that everyone else in the store was Chinese and that most of the customers only spoke Chinese! The people in the store had all laughed good-naturedly, but their kind laughter had only emphasized the fact that she still didn't know enough about the city to survive.

"I've been thinking of getting a job, too," Chrissy wrote. "The only trouble is, I don't know what kind of job I'm qualified for." Even the beginner's jobs called for people over eighteen. And the fast-food restaurants close to home were not hiring right now, although she had filled out application after application. In fact, she was fast beginning to think that she wasn't good enough even to get the worst-paying job in the city.

Chrissy sighed again. *Maybe I should never have come back here*, she thought. *Maybe I've already spent enough time in California. I know that I don't really belong here. The trouble is that I'm not even sure I belong back home anymore,*

but a least I know about farms. I'm useful there.
People would hire me—they wouldn't look at me
like I was a cockroach every time I went to see
about a job.

She began writing again. "If you have any
suggestions of things I might be able to do, write
me," she scribbled quickly. "I'm just not sure what
I could do in the city. I don't have any special
experience like Caroline has with music. I don't
think city people would appreciate my experience with hogs, and I've never done any work
except around the farm and baby-sitting. I suppose I could always do that again, but it doesn't
pay as well as real work. It might be fun to work
with little kids, and I could always do my homework when they were asleep, and I do need some
extra money if I want to see all the sights of
California before I come home."

A door slammed down the hall.

"Chrissy, where are you?" Caroline called.

Before Chrissy could answer, Caroline burst
into the bedroom. "Oh, there you are," she said,
her face glowing. "I've had the best time! Chrissy,
it was wonderful. They are the nicest people. Mr.
Simon says I can work however much I want to,
and he understands about homework."

"That's great, Cara," Chrissy said with as much
enthusiasm as she could muster.

"And there's this boy there, Chrissy," Caroline
went on, her voice softer now. "He's got this
sparkle in his eyes that reminds me so much of
Luke . . . ." Her voice trailed off, as if her mind

were in another place, another time. Then she seemed to snap back to reality as she continued, "Anyway, he's a senior over at Lincoln High, and he plays the drums in the Youth Symphony *and* with a rock band. Isn't that exciting! He says all sorts of rock stars come into the store!"

Caroline broke off suddenly and looked at her cousin. "I'm sorry," she said. "That was pretty dumb of me, to come bursting in here bragging about my job when you haven't found one yet."

"It's okay," said Chrissy. "I'm really glad for you, Cara. "And I'm very envious about this rock drummer. When do I get to meet him?"

"Never, if I have anything to do with it," Caroline said with a grin. "I know your powers of flirtation, Chrissy Madden."

"I do not flirt," Chrissy said. "In fact, I'm beginning to believe I don't do anything well."

Caroline came and perched on the arm of her chair. "Hey, cheer up," she said. "This isn't like you to be so down."

Chrissy nodded. "I'm just finding it hard to get used to being a failure," she said. "Back home I knew what I was good at. I was used to succeeding—I was head cheerleader, and the other kids looked up to me, and I had a supercute boyfriend, and—"

"Are you having second thoughts about Ben?" Caroline interrupted.

Chrissy chewed on her lip. "It's having too much time to sit around and think," she said. "I keep asking myself if I made a big mistake, and what if he was the only person who's ever going to fall in love with me."

Caroline laughed. "Oh, come on. You know you have no trouble getting guys. Now I, on the other hand, am really a hopeless case."

"You? You got Luke to fall in love with you!" Chrissy blurted out before she realized that she should have kept her mouth shut. "He was the best catch in the whole county."

Caroline's eyes took on that dreamy, faraway look. "That's what scares me, Chrissy," she said. "I can't get him out of my mind. I keep wondering if he was the big love of my life and I'll never feel this way again."

"You've got your cute drummer to help take your mind off him," Chrissy suggested.

The dreamy look stayed on Caroline's face. "I wonder," she said. "Jeff certainly is cute and nice, and working at the store stops me from moping around, but I get the feeling that Luke isn't someone I'll get over just like that."

"I get the same feeling about Ben," Chrissy said. "I know that every boy I meet from now on, I'll compare to him."

There was a silence as both girls withdrew into their own private worlds. Then Chrissy burst out laughing.

"Boy, we must look like a couple of loonies," she said. "What we need is an extra-large hot-fudge sundae!"

Caroline brightened up, too. "Let's go down to Mama's," she suggested. "My treat, okay?"

"Okay," Chrissy said, jumping up from her chair. "As long as you let me treat as soon as I've got my job."

"I'm sure you'll get something soon," Caroline said. "We'll look at the Sunday paper tomorrow. That has a huge want ad section."

"Yeah, full of ads for people aged eighteen or over with fifty years of experience!" Chrissy said. "The only thing I have experience in is baby-sitting, and I really don't want to work for a dollar an hour."

Caroline looked at her cousin as if she were crazy. "A dollar an hour?" she asked. "More like five dollars an hour."

"Five dollars?"

"You can get five dollars here, if you're lucky, but you wouldn't get less than three," she said.

"Holy cow! That's not half-bad," Chrissy exclaimed.

"But baby-sitting, Chrissy," Caroline said, wrinkling her nose. "I mean, it's not the greatest job, is it?"

"I wouldn't mind it at all," Chrissy said excitedly, "especially at five dollars an hour! I'm good with little kids. Baby-sitting is easy. I'd just have to play with the kids and feed them. Then when I tuck them in their little beds they'll look up at me with big eyes and whisper, 'We love you, Aunty Chrissy!' "

Caroline rolled her eyes. "Rather you than me," she said. "The only kids I ever baby-sat for tried to ambush me with G.I. Joe's commando unit!"

"You obviously don't have the right touch," Chrissy said. "Kids can sense my wonderful warmth and motherly charm. Besides," she added as she reached for her jacket, "I bribe them with cookies!"

Caroline laughed. "I'll wait and see what happens after your first evening of baby-sitting," she said. "I suspect that city kids grow up a lot faster than kids in Danbury, Iowa."

Chrissy paused in the doorway. "Even the brattiest city kid will find it had to resist my irresistible charm," Chrissy said. "And fortified with an ice-cream sundae, my charm should soon be working again at full strength!" she yelled as she ran down the hall ahead of Caroline, feeling better than she had all week.

Chapter 4

The next day Chrissy studied the want ads with Caroline's help. There was a long list of people who needed baby-sitters and mother's helpers, and Chrissy sat down next to the phone feeling optimistic and excited. It would be great to tell the kids at school on Monday that she had a job, too!

As she worked her way down the list, however, her depression of the past week returned. The people she talked to wanted mature women as sitters, nannies not teenage girls. She knew that parents had to be very careful when hiring someone to take care of their kids, but she couldn't understand why they wouldn't trust her.

Finally, when she had almost give up hope, she talked to Mrs. Hurst.

"I really wanted someone a little older," Mrs. Hurst said, sounding as suspicious as the other mothers. "I was thinking more of a college girl."

"Oh, but I'm very reliable," Chrissy said, "and I have had a lot of experience. I've been baby-sitting since I was eleven years old."

"Well, I have to admit I'm pretty desperate right now," Mrs. Hurst said. "I'm going back to school. . . ."

"To get your diploma? I think that's wonderful," Chrissy said, trying to sound like a bubbly, enthusiastic baby-sitter.

"To get my master's degree," came the crisp voice at the other end. "I'm trying to fit in night classes with my full-time job."

"That's wonderful," Chrissy said, a little more cautiously this time.

"So come over tomorrow afternoon, and I'll give you a try," Mrs. Hurst said. "It's important that my children like you."

"Oh, children and I always get along well together," Chrissy said.

"These are very sensitive children," Mrs. Hurst said firmly. "They don't like everybody."

So the next afternoon Chrissy went off, full of hope and confidence, to the apartment on Nob Hill, an exclusive section of San Francisco. At least she was sure of one thing—she knew how to amuse kids, and kids always liked her. This job might not pay as well as theaters or music stores, but it would be a piece of cake!

When she reached the apartment, Chrissy

found that Miranda Hurst was nothing like she had imagined. Instead of an efficient business-woman in a conservative suit, Mrs. Hurst was dressed in blue jeans and an old UC Berkeley T-shirt.

"I'm afraid I have to run," she panted as Chrissy showed up at the front door. "I forgot I have a lab class this afternoon and a lecture tonight. This is Skyler and this is Guinevere. I know you are going to relate to each other very well."

Then she was gone. Chrissy knelt down to be on the level with the small children and smiled at them "I'm Chrissy," she said. "And guess what—I stopped by at the bakery and got these for you."

She drew out two pink sugary heart cookies. The children stepped back as if they were being offered spiders.

"We can't eat those," six-year-old Skyler said.

"You mustn't have snacks between meals, then?" Chrissy went on brightly. "Okay, we'll put them in the kitchen until after dinner."

"We can't eat them at all," Guinevere said in a very serious voice for a four-year-old. "They are pink."

"You don't like pink?" Chrissy asked in confusion.

"It has red food dye in it," Skyler said crushingly. "That's a poison."

"And sugar," Guinevere added. "That makes Skyler hyperactive."

"Oh," Chrissy said. She got to her feet and looked around for inspiration. She'd never met children who wouldn't eat cookies before, and now she had to think of a new way to gain their favor. "Do you want to show me where you keep your toys?"

Two pairs of dark eyes stared coldly at Chrissy, and she felt the smile gradually fade from her lips. She tried again. "Let's go take a look at your toys, shall we?"

"I'm going to work on my computer," Skyler said, turning his back on Chrissy. As an afterthought he looked back. "Are you any good at formatting commands for Wordstar?"

"Er . . . no," Chrissy stammered.

"What sort of computer and software do you have, then?" he asked.

"Er . . . I don't have a computer."

"What do you do your homework on?" he asked, looking at his sister in amazement.

"With a pen," Chrissy said.

"You must be very poor," Skyler commented.

"Of course she's poor, that's why she has to baby-sit for us," Guinevere answered, pushing open the door to her room and taking a variety of educational toys from the shelves. "Do you have a boyfriend?" she asked Chrissy.

"Er . . . Not right now," she stammered. "We broke up."

"Because of sex, right?" Guinevere asked, calmly tipping out wooden puzzle pieces onto the ceramic tiled floor.

"Er . . . no. . . ." Chrissy stammered. *Holy cow*

she thought. *Cara wasn't kidding when she said city kids grow up fast.*

Guinevere looked scornful. "Don't be embarrassed. Miranda says that so many people have hangups about sex," she said. "She's a counselor."

"Miranda?"

"My mother. She likes us to call her Miranda."

Chrissy looked at the small face suspiciously. She was almost beginning to suspect that Guinevere was, in fact not a four-year-old child but a ventriloquist's dummy, opening her mouth while other people's words spewed out.

"What do you want to play?" she asked.

"I don't know, I'm bored with all my toys," Guinevere said, tipping multicolored tiles to join the puzzle pieces.

"How about playing house? Chrissy suggested. "I always liked to play house when I was your age."

"Okay," Guinevere said, opening a toy chest and dragging out several dolls. "I'll be the Mommy, and I'm a lawyer. These are my babies, and I'm taking them to the day-care center." She thrust the dolls into Chrissy's arms. "You're the day-care lady, and you get to look after them."

Chrissy gave a sigh of frustration. "I think we should put some of these things away," she suggested, starting to stack the wooden tiles in their box again.

"I think I feel like drawing," Guinevere said, ignoring Chrissy's suggestion. "I think I'll draw a giraffe with my crayons."

"That's nice," Chrissy said, delighted that Guinevere was finally going to do something normal.

"There," Guinevere said triumphantly after a few minutes. "Do you like my giraffe?"

Chrissy turned and opened her mouth in horror. "Guinevere—you scribbled on the walls!" she yelled.

"It isn't scribble. It's a giraffe. That's where I wanted to draw my giraffe today," Guinevere said with just the trace of a mischievous smile on her little face.

"But your mom will be so mad," Chrissy said, jumping up and running into the kitchen. "We'll have to try and wipe it off before she gets back, and I know what crayon's like. It never comes off. . . ."

She came running back with every variety of cleaning material clutched in her arms. Guinevere sat on the floor, Indian style, to watch her.

"Oh no, I don't know which of these things to use," Chrissy said. "I wonder if scouring powder or spray cleaner would be best."

"Don't make such a fuss," Guinevere said. She picked up a rag. "Miranda had the walls painted with special paint so I can wipe my pictures right off again. She knows I like to draw on walls."

"Oh, I see. Uh, good idea," Chrissy stammered, trying not to show her anger. She began wiping the crayon from the wall.

"Don't wipe him off yet!" Guinevere whined. "I

like my giraffe. Now I've got to draw another one."

Chrissy went in defeat to sit on a miniature chair. The evening was becoming a nightmare. She had thought that baby-sitting would be an easy way to earn money. Now she wasn't so sure. She hadn't realized that San Francisco children would be so different from kids back home.

"Let's go see what Skyler is doing," she said to Guinevere.

"He hates it if you interrupt the middle of one of his programs," Guinevere said. "He knows bok fu, you know. He can kill a person if he wants to. I do it, too, but I'm only a white belt still. Watch. Ha! Ha!" She kicked out her foot forcefully only inches from Chrissy's middle.

"Very good," Chrissy said, stepping back uneasily. "I can see you're an expert."

"I'm not an expert," Guinevere said, giving her a withering look. "I'm a white belt. Don't you know anything? Skyler is already a purple belt. He goes to tournaments. So does Miranda."

Chrissy looked at the clock and saw with relief that it might be almost dinnertime for the children. "Let's put away your toys, and then we'll wash up for dinner," she said. "Skyler, time to put away your things."

Skyler's head appeared in his doorway. "I don't like to put away my things," he said calmly.

Chrissy laughed. "I'm sure you don't, but you have to clean up when you're finished playing, don't you?"

"No."

"You don't have to clear up your toys?"

"Only if I want to, and I don't want to today. Miranda says we are expressing our own personalities if we like messy rooms."

"I see," Chrissy said. "But what about school—you have to clear up after yourself at school, don't you?"

"I go to a private school," Skyler said, walking ahead of her down the hall. "We can do what we like there, too."

"Skyler does math all the time," Guinevere confided. "Three weeks of math, math, math. I think he's dumb."

"I am not dumb."

"Are too."

"Am not."

"You want to bok fu with me?"

"That's enough!" Chrissy yelled. "Sit and eat. Look, your mom has left a sandwich for each of you."

"Yuck," they said in unison.

"I'm going to make myself grilled cheese," said Skyler.

"And I'm having peanut butter and pickle," Guinevere added. "We don't have to eat stuff we don't like. That's expressing ourselves."

Chrissy could find nothing to say. She simply watched in agony as Skyler grated the cheese onto the floor, and Guinevere dipped a huge dill pickle into a jar of peanut butter. Finally she felt that she was about to explode.

"Okay. Eight o'clock. Time for bed," she said as she started to put away the food and dirty dishes.

"We stay up as late as we want," Skyler declared. "Sometimes I go to bed after Miranda."

"Not tonight you don't," Chrissy said.

"But that's expressing myself," Skyler replied as if challenging Chrissy to top that reasoning.

"And I'm expressing myself, too," Chrissy said, glaring at the children. She pointed to the doorway. "Go brush your teeth and then go to bed right now. Both of you. Am I expressing myself clearly enough?"

Her voice was so fierce and her face so terrifying that both of them scampered from the kitchen without another word. It wasn't until they reached the bathroom that Chrissy heard Skyler say loudly to Guinevere, "Gee, she's mean!"

"Did you have any problems with the children?" Miranda Hurst asked when she came back around ten that night.

"Everything was fine," Chrissy said hesitantly.

"Oh, I'm so glad," Miranda Hurst sighed. "Some sitters just do not understand how creative and sensitive my children are. One woman actually ruined this lovely picture that Guinevere had painted on the wall. Can you imagine? It can damage their little psyches so easily."

If I stick round here much longer, I will want to damage more than their little psyches, Chrissy thought. *This is definitely one job I only keep until I find something better.*

Chapter 5

To Chrissy's surprise, Mrs. Hurst kept calling her to baby-sit. She couldn't believe that the children hadn't "expressed themselves" by refusing to have her back. While she was not thrilled at the prospect of more evenings with them, at least it was money in her pocket, which was better than none at all.

Every day she looked hopefully in the evening paper for a job that would take her away from the Hursts, but every day she was painfully reminded that she wasn't qualified for much besides baby-sitting, and now she even doubted her qualification for that! Then, just when she thought she would have to take bok fu classes in order to keep Skyler and Guinevere under control, fate stepped in, in the form of a beautiful golden dog.

She was returning home one Monday evening after a particularly hard session of baby-sitting. Skyler had been in a bad temper because he couldn't get his program to create a three-dimensional spaceship. He was mad at himself, mad at his computer, and especially mad at Chrissy because she couldn't help him. As she left the house she felt completely drained, ready to curl up into a ball and go to sleep.

"I don't need money that much," she muttered as she walked down from the heights of expensive Nob Hill back to the comfortable pastel apartments and houses of the lower hillside. "I'd rather never eat pizza again and never have any new clothes than face those terrible kids again. It's about time someone brought a suit for baby-sitter abuse! That mother will never believe how bad her kids are until she comes home one night and finds the baby-sitter lying bok fu'd to death in the front hall!"

Suddenly, Chrissy's daydream was interrupted by loud shouts ahead of her. She looked up just in time to see a large yellow dog hurtling toward her, his leash trailing behind him. As he passed Chrissy, she made a brave grab at the leash. The dog's strength nearly pulled her down the street with him, but she hung on grimly until the big dog looked around in surprise to find that his feet were moving but he was going nowhere.

"Easy boy," she said soothingly. "What's your

hurry? Come here. You didn't want to run under a car, did you?" The big curly dog started to wag his brush of a tail and lick Chrissy's outstretched hand. She laughed and ran her hands through his thick fur. "You bad thing, running away like that," she crooned. "Now we'd better find who you belong to. Come on, let's go walkies." She attempted to drag him back down the hill, but it was like dragging a sack of lead. The dog simply would not move. He curled his legs under his body and lay down on the sidewalk, wagging his tail vigorously and looking at Chrissy with big brown eyes. She began to giggle as she squatted down beside him.

"You are a clown," she said, "but you can't lie there all night. Come on, up you get." This time she succeeded in coaxing him to his feet, but instead of walking down the hill, the dog leaped at Chrissy, nearly knocking her backward, and started licking her face.

"Get down, you big old softie," she said, pushing him away with a giggle.

"Oh, thank heavens, you've got him," a voice called.

Chrissy looked up to see a young man, bright red in the face from having run up the hill and breathing very heavily, stagger the last few steps toward her. "I thought he was a goner this time," the man said, giving her a friendly smile.

"Oh, this is your dog," Chrissy said, pushing down the friendly animal with her knee as he attempted to jump up again. "I'm glad I found you. I was wondering what happened to the owner."

"I'm not the owner, thank heavens," the young man said with a big grin. "He's just in my care at the moment. He has a history as an escape artist. They ought to have called him Houdini, not Honey." The dog began wagging his tail at the sound of his name. The young man leaned across and took the leash from Chrissy. The dog pulled and tried to get back to her again, panting and whining.

"Hey, he really likes you," the man said. "You've made a big hit."

"Most dogs like me," Chrissy said shyly. "I'm good with animals, better than I am with people, I guess."

The man began to ruffle the dog's fur. "Come on, you dreadful creature," he said affectionately. "You think you've got some sympathy now, don't you. You think she'll protect you so that you don't have to come with me after all." He looked up at Chrissy and grinned. "I only had the car door open for a second," he said, "but that was all he needed."

Chrissy patted the soft fur behind the dog's ears. "He seems like a pretty fast dog," she said.

"And strong, too," the man added. "How did you manage to hang on to him?"

Chrissy looked at the man's tanned face, unruly brown hair, and athletic body dressed in old blue jeans and a T-shirt, and decided that he wasn't like other city people and wouldn't laugh if she told him about the farm. "I've had experience with farm animals, she replied. "I'm used to being dragged around by horses and cows."

"You've lived on a farm?" he asked with interest.

Chrissy nodded. "My family still lives on a farm in Iowa. I'm just here for a few more months, staying with my cousin."

The young man's eyes sparkled. "Listen," he said hesitantly, "I don't suppose you'd like a job, would you? I could really do with some experienced help."

"You train dogs or something?" she asked with interest.

He laughed. "Not exactly. I'm a vet."

"A veterinarian?" Chrissy heard the words come out as a squeak. "But you don't look . . . I mean you don't seem . . ." She paused, blushing.

"You mean I don't look old enough to be a vet," he finished for her, and laughed easily. "I know I don't look old enough. I was still getting half fare on the buses when I was in college! I guess it's my innocent, healthy life-style that has kept me young-looking!"

"Wow, so you really are a vet?" Chrissy asked.

"James Garrison, D.V.M. I could show you my diploma," he said, still laughing. "So how about it—would you be interested in an after-school job, or are you also really older than you look and already a bank executive and mother of three?"

Chrissy giggled. "I'm Chrissy Madden, and I'm

a high school junior," she said, "and you don't know how much I'd love to work for you. I've been looking for a job for what seems like ages. Right now I'm stuck baby-sitting for a family of monsters. Animals are so much easier. I don't know why I didn't think to look for a job with a vet."

"It wouldn't be all fun," Dr. Garrison said, his face serious again. "My assistants have to do all the dirty stuff, too—hose out the animal pens, wash out feeding bowls, clean up unspeakable animal messes . . .

"I'm used to all that," Chrissy said. "I've even mucked out the neighbor's pig sty, and nothing gets more gross than pigs, I can tell you."

"Don't I know," he said. "I did part of my internship in a farm practice. Dogs and cats are very clean and dainty compared to cows and pigs. Look, Chrissy—my office is down at the bottom of the hill. Do you want to come over tomorrow after school and I can show you the job?"

"Sure!" Chrissy replied. What could be more perfect than actually getting paid to work with animals? And to have a cute boss like Dr. Garrison, too!

"Good. I can't believe my luck in running into you, Chrissy," he said, rummaging through his pockets. "Ah, here it is—my business card, so you'll know where to come tomorrow." He handed the card to Chrissy. "I'll see you tomorrow, then, if I can ever get this brute back to my office. Come on, Honey. Heel!" He pulled the dog into place beside him. Honey followed reluctantly, looking back hopefully at Chrissy. Dr. Garrison also turned to look back at her. "I think he knows he's going to get his w-o-r-m medicine," he called. "He doesn't like it. See you tomorrow, then! Any time will do."

Then he was gone, swallowed up into the traffic at the cross street. Chrissy stood staring after him, remembering the good-looking man, the big friendly dog, and wondering if the whole thing had been a fantasy. *Tomorrow I'll find out for sure*, she thought. *I do hope it's all true. Working for a vet would be my dream job, but working for a vet who looks like that would be heaven! I can't wait to tell Cara about this.*

Chapter 6

As it turned out, that night Caroline did not arrive home until the middle of dinner.

"Sorry I'm late, everyone," she called, breezing into the kitchen and sliding into her seat, "but you'll never guess what happened! I sold a piano! Imagine—me, selling a real piano. I was so excited when he handed over the check that my hands were trembling."

"I hope you got proper identification on that check," her father said.

"Of course I did, Daddy," Caroline said. "I did just what Mr. Simon wanted me to do. Besides, he looked like such a nice man, and he was buying it for his little daughter."

Her father laughed. "You should know that how people look does not mean a thing. A big city like this is full of con men who all look like nice, regular guys."

Caroline patted his hand. "I'm not stupid, Daddy. I know that," she said. "I got his ID, and what's more, the piano is not being delivered until Thursday, which gives us time to verify everything. I intend to be a good business-woman, and I'm not going to be taken in by anybody."

She grinned across at Chrissy as she helped herself to salad. "So how were the monsters tonight? How many times were you karate chopped?" she asked.

"It's bok fu'd," Chrissy corrected. "I think it's more like boxing and karate combined. It looks dangerous enough for me to stay out of Skyler's way when he's mad."

Caroline looked at her with sympathy. "Poor old Chrissy," she said. "I do hope you find a better job soon. I want you to find a job like mine, a job that's fun every minute!"

Chrissy opened her mouth to make her an-nouncement, then shut it again. She'd better wait to make sure the job was real. If she told Caroline now, and Dr. Garrison took back his offer tomor-row for some reason, then Caroline would feel even more sorry for her and tell her she was too trusting and not city wise enough. So she simply nodded to Caroline and busied herself with scooping up the last of her peas. She knew that Caroline was being nice and kind to her, but her pity was difficult to deal with.

It's really hard when you've been the sort of person who has always succeeded, she thought as she watched Caroline going back to telling all the exciting things that had happened at the store. *Back home I was always the one who did things . . . and people cheered. And now, suddenly, I'm the one who can't do anything right!* She glanced back down at her plate as Caroline caught her gaze. *If only I can sit here tomorrow and announce my news! If only . . .*

The next day, Chrissy rushed out of the school building as soon as the bell rang. She ran up and down the hills all the way to the address on Dr. Garrison's card. Finally she stopped outside a large friendly-looking house, with a sign on the lawn reading "Garrison's Veterinary Hospital." Suddenly, she felt nervous. What if she was disappointed? When at last she forced herself to step inside, she was greeted by a stone-faced, blue-haired woman.

"Can I help you?" the woman asked in a sharp voice. "Y-yes please," Chrissy stammered. "I'm here to see Dr. Garrison."

"Well, what's the problem?" asked the woman.

"There is no problem," Chrissy replied.

"No cat with an ingrown toenail or canary with laryngitis?"

Chrissy shook her head. "No, nothing like that. Dr. Garrison asked me to come in this afternoon." She didn't want to mention the job, just in case he'd changed his mind.

"Well, the doctor is in with a patient now," the woman said, then pointed to a group of chairs against the opposite wall. "You can wait there."

The waiting seemed eternal. There were no animal patients to play with in the waiting room, so Chrissy read every poster on heartworm and feline enteritis several times before a man cuddling a tiny kitten finally came out a side door.

"Who's next, Annie?" a voice called.

"Just a young person to see you, sir," Annie had answered.

Then, to Chrissy's utter delight, Dr. Garrison's unruly head of curls poked around the door. "Chrissy!" he said. "I'm so glad you came. You must have thought I acted so strange last night, but I'm not a weirdo at all. Annie can vouch for that, can't you, Annie?"

Annie did not smile. "I'm not so sure about that, sir," she said with a sniff.

"Chrissy is coming to help us out," Dr. Garrison said happily. "She's going to be assistant on the days Roger can't get here."

"Anything would be better than that boy," Annie said with another sniff.

"Oh, come on, Annie. He means well," Jim Garrison said with a grin.

Annie sniffed again. "A walking disaster area. That's what he is!"

Dr. Garrison put an arm on Chrissy's shoulder. It was a friendly arm, but it made her knees go instantly weak. He seemed unaware of the effect he was having as he led her through to his office.

"Let's get you fitted in a lab coat, then I'll show you where things are. Just watch and get the hang of things today, okay?"

"Oh, I don't mind getting right down to work," she said. "I'm used to working hard on our farm at home."

"Great!" Jim Garrison beamed. "Then maybe I can have you clean out the empty kennels after the patients have been picked up."

Later that afternoon, Chrissy sighed contentedly. She had spent an exhausting but exciting few hours helping Dr. Garrison, watching him give shots to a puppy, set the broken leg of a big St. Bernard, and prescribe medications for a dozen more animals—even a tiny mouse! Nothing could spoil her complete happiness—not Annie's unfriendliness, not even the prospect of sweeping out the dirty kennels. In half an hour she would be able to go home and break her news over dinner. "Guess what, everybody," she would say. "I'm not baby-sitting anymore. I'm a veterinarian's assistant. How about that?"

And they'd all look impressed and tell her how smart she was to find such a good job.

Chrissy glanced down at her white lab coat. It made her feel very special—almost as if she were a vet herself.

Just then she heard footsteps coming down the hall and looked up to see Dr. Garrison walking toward her. "You can lock up, can't you, Chrissy?" he said, pressing a bunch of keys into her hand. "Oh, and why don't you call me Jim? Dr. Garrison sounds like an old guy, and I want us to be good friends."

He winked at her, and Chrissy found herself wondering how much meaning she could put into that. After all, he was already a doctor, and she was just a high school kid. But he was so cute, and he was so nice to her. He treated her almost as if they were the same age.

Don't go reading too much into that wink, Chrissy Madden, she warned herself. *You don't really think a grown-up doctor is going to be interested in you! But he did ask me to call him Jim*, she reminded herself. *Even Annie doesn't call him by his first name. That must mean he thinks of me as something special. . . .*

She picked up her broom and walked past the occupied kennels, pausing to pat the nose of every dog she could reach. She started to sweep out cages, humming as she worked. Then she went to get a pail of hot water and a mop, determined to leave the whole area sparkling clean. She wanted Dr. Garrison to come in the next morning and be impressed. "How about that?" he'd say to Annie. "She's a really good worker, isn't she?" And Annie would have to admit that she was.

She washed out the first cage and was just carrying the heavy bucket down the hall to the next when she heard a noise. It sounded like a door being rattled, as if somebody wanted to get in. She went and peered into the front office, but she didn't see anyone outside the frosted glass door. She walked back again very cautiously, suddenly aware that she was alone in the building and it was getting dark.

"Will you stop worrying," she told herself severely. "It was probably just a noise from next door. You are perfectly safe here. The front door is locked, and the back door is locked. Who would want to break in, anyway? No burglar would be dumb enough to try it until he was sure everyone had gone home. There's not even anything to steal. Besides, you could always let out a couple of dogs to defend you. . . ."

Somewhat reassured, she walked back down the hall. It seemed very dark and gloomy now, and the front office looked like a pinprick of light at the end of a very long tunnel. The dogs were alert, too. Chrissy saw them listening, ears pricked, noses pressed against the wire of their cages.

They heard something, too, she thought. *Stop it, Chrissy*! she scolded herself. *It's probably just someone walking by on the sidewalk. You won't be much good at this job if you're going to have hysterics every time you're left alone*!

Then the big German shepherd in the nearest cage gave a low growl. Chrissy felt her skin crawling. She stood in the hallway, peering down toward the front office, every muscle tense and ready for flight. Then, right behind her, came a low creaking sound. She turned cautiously in time to see the door to the supply room opening slowly. The dogs were barking wildly now.

Chrissy wanted to run, but her feet wouldn't move. She wanted to scream, but no sound would come out of her mouth. She felt powerless, as if she were in the middle of a nightmare. As she watched in horror, a hand came around the door, and a tall, thin figure sneaked into the hall.

At last Chrissy found her voice and screamed. At the same time, she heard another scream blending with hers and realized that it was coming from the intruder. The intruder leaped back and bumped into the wall, knocking over Chrissy's bucket of water

The clatter echoed through the hallway as the bucket flew against the tiled walls, slopping everywhere. The dogs barked even louder and the intruder cowered, frozen against the wall, staring at Chrissy as if she were a ghost.

"What are you doing here? You nearly scared the daylights out of me," said a very shaky voice. He glanced down at the bucket. "Now look what you made me do."

"Me scare the daylights out of you?" Chrissy demanded, sensing that this was no criminal. The intruder walked forward into the light, and she could see now that he was a very tall, slim boy with hair flopping forward across his forehead and earnest eyes behind heavy-rimmed glasses. She glared at him. "How do you think I felt?" she asked. "I thought my heart was going to stop."

"I didn't expect to find anybody here," said the boy. "I know Annie always goes home at five-thirty. What are you doing?"

"I was trying to clean out these kennels until you kicked over my water," she said. "I hope you've got a good explanation."

"I'm looking for a chemistry book," the boy said.

"Then you're looking in the wrong place, buster," Chrissy said angrily. With the relief of finding the intruder harmless and herself in one piece, Chrissy felt her temperature rising dangerously. "For your information, this is neither a bookstore nor a school."

"No, you don't understand," the boy stammered. "I must have left my chemistry book here yesterday evening. I didn't notice it was missing until I started on my homework tonight, so I thought I'd just pop in through the window in the supply room and see if it was here. I bet it's in the drawer in Annie's desk. That's where she usually puts things I leave lying around." He started to walk down the hall toward the office. "Hi, Bonzo, old pal. Hi, Cuddles. Hi, Zozo," he said as he passed each cage. He reached the office and pulled open the bottom drawer in Annie's desk, taking out a large tattered book. "Yup, here it is," he said. "That's one good thing. Now I won't get an F on the chemistry test tomorrow." He looked at Chrissy and smiled for the first time. "So what are you doing here?" he asked. "Are you working here now?"

"Oh, no, I thought I'd just come and clean up for fun," Chrissy said dryly. "The door was open, and I thought, Why not? It seemed like a good way to pass an evening. Made a change from movies and pizza."

The boy looked embarrassed. "So you are working here," he said. "I'm sorry. Jim never tells me anything."

"Jim?"

"Dr. Garrison. Everyone calls him Jim."

"Oh, I see."

"I'm Roger Farley," the boy said, sticking out a hand for her to shake. "I work here, too. Didn't Jim tell you?

"Jim didn't, but I heard him talking to Annie about you," Chrissy said.

Roger made a face. "I can imagine what she said. She doesn't like me. She thinks I'm always causing trouble, just because I happen to be a little accident prone when she's around. I don't know why it is, but I tend to bump into things when people yell at me!"

Chrissy grinned and relaxed. "She didn't seem to like me, either. She looked at me as though I were a stray cockroach," she said.

"She doesn't like anybody," Roger said, "but she worked for Jim's father for about twenty years, so he's stuck with her. He inherited her with the practice. What did you say your name was?"

"I didn't. It's Chrissy," she said.

"Nice to meet you, Chrissy," Roger said with a shy smile. "And I'm glad to have a kid of my own age working here. I'm crazy about animals, are you? I'm planning to be a veterinarian myself.

I've got to get into a good college first, though." He hugged his chemistry book to him, and his eyes sparkled through his dark-rimmed spectacles.

"I like animals, too," Chrissy agreed.

"Great! What's your favorite animal?" Roger asked, moving close to her and resting his arm on the wall beside her head. Chrissy felt uncomfortable with Roger standing so close—after all, they'd only just met.

Then she smiled to herself. If he really wanted to know her favorite animal, he was in for a real shock. "I like pigs best" Chrissy said, looking at Roger for a reaction.

"I hear they are very intelligent," he said, beaming. "In fact, some people even house-train them and keep them as pets. Where have you had experience with pigs?"

"I come from a farm," Chrissy mumbled. She moved away from him to retrieve the mop and hoped he would get the hint.

But Roger's eyes lit up. "No kidding? Wow, that's great. I'm really interested in working with big animals. Most of the dogs and cats we get here are so pampered and neurotic. I've done some work with cows—now that's a soothing sort of animal. You have any cows on your farm?"

"A few," Chrissy said. "Now, if you'll excuse me. I really better clean up this water before the puddle reaches the kennels I've already done."

"Oh, let me help you," he said, reaching to take the mop. "It was my fault, wasn't it? Give me the mop, and we can sweep it down the drain in the supply room."

"No, Roger, it's okay. I can do it," Chrissy said, trying to wrestle the mop from him.

"Oh, but I insist—it will go much more quickly with two," He tugged at the mop once more and Chrissy gave up the struggle at the same moment.

"Okay, take it," she said, then watched as Roger went flying backward with the mop, staggered to regain his balance, then put his foot into the bucket.

"Roger, watch out!" Chrissy yelled too late as the dogs began barking again.

Roger shook his foot. "Now there's a pail on my foot!" he said with a sigh. "How to impress a new girl. First give her heart failure, then kick over a bucket and get it stuck on your foot. Nice going, Roger!"

He looked so funny, staring down with such big eyes at his bucket-encased foot. Chrissy tried not to giggle but couldn't help it. She leaned against the wall, giggling helplessly.

"Do you think you could help me get this thing off?" he asked politely. "I'm really not enjoying this too much."

"Oh, Roger—you look so funny!" she said between bouts of laughter.

"I guess I do," he admitted seriously, "but I really don't want to walk home three blocks with a bucket on my foot, so please help pull it off."

His face was so wistful, like a little boy's, that

Chrissy forced herself to stop giggling. "Okay, Roger," she said, kneeling down beside him. "Now, hold on to the bars and don't let go. I'm going to pull the bucket. Ready . . ." Roger nodded. "One . . . two . . . three!" Chrissy pulled, and the bucket came flying off with a clang.

"Thank heavens for that," he muttered. "Now, let me get you some more hot water. I'm really sorry for all the trouble I've caused. . . ."

"It's okay," Chrissy said. "I can do it, honestly."

"But I want to—:

"Now, Roger, don't start that again," Chrissy said severely. "If you get any more buckets on your foot, I won't take them off. You'll have to wear them forever. Now go do your chemistry homework. I don't want you to get an F on your test."

"Neither do I," he said. "Thanks, Chrissy. I'm glad we met. I hope you don't think that I'm always a klutz—I do have my normal moments, you know."

He gave her such a hopeful smile that she smiled back. In fact, she only just stopped herself in time from confessing to him that she also had her klutzy moments. Instead she said briskly, "I'll let you out the front door. You might get stuck if you tried to climb out of the window again, then you'd have the crowning embarrassment of being pulled out by the fire department."

"Whatever you say," he said amiably. "You're probably right. The way things are going this evening, anything is possible." As Chrissy unlocked the front door, Roger said simply, "That's why I like animals, I guess." They take you for what you are, and they don't care if you happen to be a klutz." He stepped out into the warm evening air. "Bye, Chrissy," he said, then he walked off with long strides. Chrissy watched him go before she closed the door again.

Chapter 7

"Chrissy, is that you?" Caroline called as Chrissy pushed open the front door. "Where have you been? It's after dark, and I knew you weren't scheduled to baby-sit tonight—I even called Tracy to find out if you were with her. To tell you the truth, I was kind of worried."

"Well, I did not get lost," Chrissy said, sweeping down the hall into their bedroom. "I did not get mixed up with weird people. I did not even get on the wrong bus. Contrary to popular expectation, I did something right for once!"

"You found a job, or a cute guy? Which?" Caroline asked excitedly.

"Both, actually," Chrissy said, a smug smile creeping across her face.

Caroline jumped in front of Chrissy, blocking

her way. "Come on, tell me everything," she insisted.

Chrissy paused for a moment, then quickly dodged around her cousin and leaped onto her bed. "You are now looking at a real veterinarian's assistant, complete with white lab coat," she said grandly.

"Chrissy, that's wonderful!" Caroline exclaimed. "That's the perfect job for you. How did you ever find it?"

"I caught a runaway dog," Chrissy said. "He was escaping en route to get his worm medicine treatment. The vet was so grateful that he offered me the job."

"Terrific! Now, let me guess—there's a guy working for the vet?"

"Correct."

"And he's really cute?"

"Not what I'd call cute."

"I thought you said there was a cute guy?"

"There is," she said. "The vet is the cute one."

Caroline laughed. "Aiming a little high, aren't we, Chrissy?"

"Not at all, Jim's a very young vet."

"Not young enough to be interested in high school juniors," Caroline said with a smile.

"He doesn't treat me like I'm just a high school junior," Chrissy said. "Anyway, we'll see. I'm having fun, and I love the job, and Jim is terrific, so I'm happy."

"And I'm really happy for you, Chrissy," Caroline said. "Now we both have great jobs."

"And how is Jeff?" Chrissy asked.

"He's really nice," Caroline said. "He knows so much about music, and he's very considerate . . ."

"But not cute enough?"

"I guess he's cute," Caroline said thoughtfully. She nodded. "Yes, he's cute all right."

"But he's not interested in you?"

"Oh, yes, he seems very interested," Caroline said. "He's made several hints about concerts he'd like to go to. . . ."

"So?"

"I don't know, Chrissy. He's very nice. . . ."

"You already said that." Chrissy laughed. "Are you saying he doesn't give you goose bumps?"

Caroline's cheeks colored. "I guess I'm not ready for another relationship yet," she said. "Jeff reminds me a lot of Luke, and I guess I'm hoping that I'll start feeling a little of that magic I used to feel around Luke. But I don't feel it yet. In fact, every time I'm alone with Jeff, I find myself thinking of Luke even more. Why can't I stop thinking about him, Chrissy?"

Chrissy went to sit next to her cousin. "Caroline, you were the one who said the relationship had to end, because nothing could come of it. You two will always be worlds apart. You don't want to go live in Iowa, and he doesn't really want to come to the city."

Caroline gave a big sigh. "I know," she said. "It's just that I want a miracle to happen, I guess. I keep hoping that Luke will show up one day, transformed into a California boy with surfer shorts. I know it's not going to happen, and I know I might not even like him if he were somebody else, but that's what I dream about."

"I know how you feel," Chrissy said. "I sometimes dream about things being different with Ben. Sometimes I wish that everything were back the way it was before. A really special person doesn't come around too often. It's sad to have to give him up."

"I guess I'll get over him in time," Caroline said. "I know that nothing can come of it, so I had better learn to forget and concentrate on boys I can have. Maybe I will go to a concert with Jeff. After all, I do need a date for the junior prom!"

"Me, too," said Chrissy. "Hey, do you think my vet would come with me?"

Caroline started to laugh. "Chrissy, I'm sure he is way past junior proms. Why don't you come down to earth and start looking for a nice, normal boyfriend? There are three thousand students in our school, and half of those are boys. That's a good selection. Start working on it."

"I don't know," Chrissy said with a dreamy sigh. "Somehow older men appeal to me much more than boys. Boys are so awkward and clumsy, and older men are so smooth and confident. I wonder how it would feel to be the first girl ever to bring a doctor to the junior prom."

Caroline laughed and gave her a friendly push. "You are a dodo, you know that?"

Chrissy put on her best superior look. "You might just be surprised, young woman. Don't forget that I am a very sophisticated, mature sixteen-year-old. I know a lot about life! I've been around. . . ."

Caroline went on giggling. "Oh, sure—all the way from Danbury, Iowa, to Des Moines and back! That's really seeing the world."

Chrissy's face didn't change. "Knowing about life is merely a state of mind," she said. "It's being completely at ease, knowing one is in command of anything. . . ." She sank backward as she talked, meaning to lean against the wall next to her bed. Instead she landed on the floor with a large clunk and a little squeak.

Caroline's giggles doubled in intensity. Chrissy gave her a withering look. "Okay, who moved the bed?" she asked.

"I guess I did when I vacuumed this afternoon," Caroline said, catching her breath. "I'm sorry. I only moved it maybe a foot or so away from the wall. I didn't think that would make any difference to a person like you who's been around and is in command of everything." Caroline cracked up again, and tears came to her eyes, she was laughing so hard.

"Very funny," Chrissy said, scowling at her cousin from the floor.

"Sorry, Chrissy," Caroline said between giggles, "but you must admit—things do seem to happen to you, especially when you're trying hard to be your sophisticated best!"

An image of Roger crossed Chrissy's mind—his embarrassment at getting his foot stuck when he

obviously wanted to make a good impression
with a new girl. *I shouldn't have laughed at him*,
she thought. She reached out a hand to Caroline.
"Now, if you would kindly help me off the floor,
I'm going to get my dinner." She acted all huffy as
Caroline pulled her to her feet, but on her way to
the kitchen her sense of humor took over, and
she found herself laughing, too.

The next day, as she walked to the veterinary
office after school, Chrissy recalled what she had
said to Caroline about Jim Garrison. She knew
she had laid the whole thing on a little thick, and
she had to admit that she had enjoyed being able
to go one better than the fabulous Jeff and the
exciting music store.

It'd be great if Jim really was interested in me,
she thought as she neared the office. *I mean, he
did ask me to work for him, and he did put his
arm around me when he took me to the supply
room. And then he winked when he said he
wanted to be good friends. But maybe he's just
being friendly, and all these things don't really
mean anything. Maybe I let my fantasizing run
away with me. One thing I do know is that I can't
let him know how I feel. He's got to make the first
move.*

Annie greeted her with the same sniff and
frown as the day before. "Oh, it's you," she said,
giving the impression that she never expected
Chrissy to show up again after one day's work.
"Dr. G is in the back somewhere, sorting through

a new batch of medications that just arrived."

"I'll go give him a hand," Chrissy offered with a smile. Although Annie's look implied that Chrissy's hand wouldn't be much help, Chrissy found herself almost bursting with anticipation as she pushed open the door of the supply room and saw a lab-coated figure standing at the sink.

"I'm here," she called brightly. "How about putting me to work?"

"Oh, great, there's a million and one things that need doing," the figure said, turning into the light.

"Oh," Chrissy said, her voice showing her disappointment. "It's you, Roger. I thought you were Dr. Garrison."

"Jim's out checking Buffy Baxter's leg," he said. "We just took stitches out of a nasty cut." The way he said it sounded as if he and Jim had just removed the dog's stitches together. "But I expect I can find you something to do," he continued, smiling at her.

Chrissy felt herself bristling with annoyance. Who did this guy think he was? "Are you my boss or something?" she asked.

Roger flushed. "I've been here awhile," he said. "I know what needs to be done. You could always start working your way through the kennels—you know, moving each animal into an empty cage while you hose down and disinfect. Did Jim show you how to do that?"

"Not yet," she said.

"Then I'll show you," Roger said.

"I see," Chrissy commented. "I get to hose down animal poop while you get to put little bottles on shelves."

"Seniority," Roger said with a grin.

"I thought Jim said I was supposed to be working on the days you weren't here," Chrissy said.

"I'm not officially here today," Roger said, "but I come down most days. I like to pop in, even though I'm not being paid. I can't really check on the progress of the animals if I don't see them on a daily basis. It means my notes aren't complete."

"Boy, you are really taking this stuff seriously," Chrissy said in surprise.

"I have to if I want to make it as a vet," he said. "Besides, this is what really interests me. I hate for these animals to suffer. Sometimes I just come down and talk to them. It makes it easier for them to accept being shut in a strange cage."

"Well then, I'd better start cleaning those cages," Chrissy said, picking up a broom.

Roger looked embarrassed. "I'm not really just handing you the horrible job," he said. "You don't know where any of this stuff goes yet, so I can get through it much quicker."

"Okay," Chrissy said, grabbing a pail. "Now, don't put your foot in this one, or I'll make you wear it for life."

"Wear what for life?" Dr. Garrison asked, stepping into the room. He grinned at Chrissy. While Roger blushed and looked at her pleadingly.

"Er, nothing, private joke," she said.

Dr. Garrison looked from one to the other. "I'm glad you two have met and are getting along so well," he said. "Rog, I know you're not officially here today, but would you mind getting started on those kennels? I want to show Chrissy where everything goes so that she feels comfortable back here."

Chrissy tried to suppress a grin of triumph as she handed Roger the broom. But after he had gone, she began to feel bad. *I hope Jim isn't starting to favor me*, she thought. *I do want him to like me, but it wouldn't be very fair to Roger if he gave me all the good jobs to do. I may have to talk to Jim about that if things go much further.*

When Roger returned to the supply room much later, she turned to face him guiltily. "Look, Roger, I'm sorry. I should have volunteered to do the kennels. You are the head honcho in the kennel cleaning department . . ."

"No, that's perfectly all right," he said. "You do need to know where everything is as quickly as possible, so that you can run and get things for Jim in emergencies. Besides, I don't mind cleaning the kennels. I get to be with the dogs and cats."

He's such a nice person, Chrissy thought in surprise. *Most boys would be furious.*

"I promise I'll do it tomorrow," Chrissy said. "How's that? Do you forgive me?"

"There was nothing to forgive," Roger said, that little-boy embarrassed look creeping over his face again. "I'm glad you've come to work here, Chrissy."

"I'm glad I have, too," Chrissy said. "I think Jim is the most fantastic boss. He really treats us like equals, and he's so good about teaching us things about the animals."

"He's a great guy," Roger said, "and I can tell he really likes you."

"You can?"

"Oh, sure. He said you were really going to brighten the place up." He paused and gave her a kind of sideways look. "He also said you were great looking."

"He did?" Now Chrissy found herself blushing.

"He was right," Roger said. "You are great looking. I bet you have lots of boyfriends."

"Not right now," Chrissy said. "I'm sort of between."

"Jim wanted to know," Roger said hastily. "He said he bet you had to fight all the boys off."

Chrissy turned away in embarrassment. "Well, I'd better see what needs to be done next," she said, walking hastily down the hall. So Jim had said she was great looking and wondered out loud about her boyfriends. Wait till she told Cara that!

Jim was nowhere to be seen. Only Annie sat, immovable as a statue, in the front office. "Dr. Garrison had to leave," she said. "House call on a pampered pet up on Nob Hill. I guess you can go home if you're all done." Then, as Chrissy turned to go, she added as an afterthought, "Oh, he left a message for you. He wanted to know if you were free Friday night."

Her face remained expressionless, even when Chrissy felt herself blushing bright scarlet. "Tell him yes," Chrissy replied without looking back, then fled into the supply room and dropped her lab coat into the laundry hamper. Her thoughts were whirling about in her mind as if on some crazy carnival ride. She didn't even hear Roger come up behind her.

"Er, look, Chrissy," he stammered. "I was wondering if you might be free Friday evening. I just happen to have a pair of tickets to a Phil Collins concert, and I thought that maybe . . ."

"Phil Collins!" Chrissy cried, then remembered that somebody else had already claimed Friday night. Even though she would have loved to see Phil Collins in concert, she would never turn down an evening with gorgeous Dr. Garrison. She wanted to say, "Sorry, Roger, old pal, but you're too late. Jim already asked me." Instead she replied, "Gee, thanks, Roger, but I'm already busy Friday evening."

Roger nodded and turned away. "Some other time, maybe?"

Chapter 8

"Here come the two working women!" Tracy called out as Caroline and Chrissy climbed the hill toward the park at lunchtime. "We thought success must have gone to your heads. We hardly see you anymore."

Chrissy looked at Caroline and grinned. "We have to be careful who we're seen with these days—our image, you know," she said, tossing her hair back. The other kids laughed. Tracy made room for the girls on the bench, and they slid into place between her and Maria. It was a clear, windy day, and Chrissy could see for miles across the blooming green hills on the other side of the bay. A fresh breeze, scented with the fragrance of a San Francisco spring swept back her long blond hair and filled her lungs. Chrissy took a deep breath and felt that she could explode with joy. She was a girl with a great job and, even more remarkable, a gorgeous boss who wanted to make a date with her for tomorrow night! Her cool city friends couldn't laugh at her now.

"How's the music store, Cara?" Justine asked. "Met any more rock stars?"

Chrissy noted that Caroline also looked confident and relaxed these days. *There's nothing like knowing you can earn a living and survive in the real world to make you feel good about yourself*, she thought.

"I've sort of gotten used to them now," Caroline said. "Jeff sold a drum pad set to the drummer from Bald Eagles yesterday."

"Really?" Justine asked, looking impressed. "The one with the shaved head, what did he look like?"

Caroline laughed. "Pretty gross, but he had a white Mercedes convertible outside!"

"And what about this Jeff guy?" asked Maria. "When do we get to meet him?"

"I don't know," Caroline said. "I'm going to a concert with him tomorrow night. Phil Collins. Should be good."

"You lucky duck," Justine said.

"Yeah, you must have been able to pull strings to get into that," Randy added. "We tried to get tickets and couldn't."

"Oh, I know a guy with a spare ticket," Chrissy said.

"You do? Who?"

"The guy I work with—he asked me to go with him."

"And you turned him down?" Maria shrieked. "He must be a real dog."

Chrissy grinned. "Let me put it this way—when I first met him, he was wearing a bucket on his foot!"

The group burst out laughing. Chrissy felt a pang of guilt as she watched them. None of them knew Roger, but it wasn't really fair to get laughs at his expense.

"Hey, Chrissy, I thought you were baby-sitting two obnoxious kids," Dino interrupted. "Where does this guy come in? Is he one of them?"

"Why don't you stay awake?" Maria said, slapping his knee. "I told you yesterday that she had got this job at a veterinarian's office."

Randy wrinkled his nose. "Is that any better than watching kids?" he asked.

"You bet it is," Chrissy said. "Even lion taming would be easier than looking after those two."

"Of course you are only interested in the animals, nothing more," Caroline added sweetly.

"What do you mean, Cara?" Tracy asked.

"I mean that having a gorgeous boss has nothing to do with her enthusiasm."

"You're working for a gorgeous guy?" asked Justine. "Wow, you sure manage to fall on your feet—money and a guy, too."

"Well, wouldn't this guy be a little old if he's a vet?" Maria asked.

"But not too old," Chrissy answered mysteriously.

"Meaning what?"

"Meaning he's already asked me out," Chrissy said smoothly.

"But he must be at least twenty-four or twenty-five to have finished all that veterinary training," Justine said in amazement. "Is this guy married, Chrissy? You better be careful. You know what old men are like about chasing young girls."

"Oh, Jim's not like that at all," Chrissy said, blushing slightly. "He's so nice, and he's really young for a vet. Right out of school, in fact. He just took over the practice from his father. That doesn't make him too much older than me."

"Wow," Justine said again. "But I still think you'd better be careful."

"I'll only go to a movie or have a meal with the guy," Chrissy said. "Maybe he's just being friendly to me, to welcome me as a new employee."

"That's what they all say," Justine said with a snort.

"Sounds like you're jealous, Justine." Tracy giggled. "I personally am very impressed. No guy in his twenties ever asked me anything except is my mother home."

"Maybe that's because you still look about twelve, Tracy," Maria said, laughing.

Tracy's elfin face puckered into a smile. "So, I'll get the last laugh. When we're all thirty, everyone will think I'm twenty!" she said. "I wish tomorrow night would hurry up and come. I'm dying to hear about your date with this guy, Chrissy."

"I'll tell you all about the parts that aren't censored," Chrissy said with a big grin as she got up to throw her wrappers into the trash bin.

All day she could do nothing but think about her date with Jim. She felt both excited and uneasy when she tried to imagine it. Was he thinking of it as a date, or was he only trying to be nice to a new employee? *I wish I was more mature and experienced*, she thought. *I wish I had dated more boys. All I know about boys comes from being around Ben, and I nearly always knew what he was thinking. But Jim . . . Jim is already a man. Am I crazy to go out with him? He seems so nice and friendly and open, but how can I tell? I wish this afternoon would hurry up and be here already, so I can find out what's on Jim's mind.*

Both Jim and Roger were sitting in the consulting room, drinking a cup of coffee when Chrissy arrived. This was one moment when she especially wished Roger were not around. How could she discuss plans with Jim with Roger listening in? Then he'd know she'd turned him down for a date with the boss, and that could make things pretty uncomfortable.

"Hi, Chrissy," Jim said easily. "Grab a cookie before Roger eats them all!" Roger tried to protest his innocence with his mouth full as Jim offered her a box of homemade chocolate-chip cookies. Chrissy took one and bit into it. "Annie

baked them, so watch out," Jim informed her
with a big grin. "I think I'm missing a bottle of
arsenic!"

Chrissy smiled back at him, thinking what a
wonderful, warm smile he had. His eyes really
sparkled when he smiled, and Chrissy could see
the beginnings of a beard on his chin if she
looked closely. "I'm making the most of my three
minutes between patients," he said, stretching
out his long legs on his stool. "It's been nonstop
rush all day. I swear every animal in the city gets
sick at the same time. I can't wait for the weekend to get away from it all. Which reminds
me . . ." He looked directly at Chrissy. "You got
my note yesterday?"

Chrissy blushed as she nodded, trying desperately to think of a way to put off this conversation
until Roger was out of the room. But Jim was
already going on, apparently unconcerned that
they were not alone.

"And you are free?" Jim asked with enthusiasm.

Chrissy nodded again, keeping her eyes well
away from Roger.

"Great," Jim said, "because I've got two tickets
for the symphony tomorrow, and we couldn't find
a baby-sitter anywhere. I know you'll love
Joshua!"

"Joshua?" Chrissy asked weakly. Why was her
dream rapidly turning into a nightmare?

"My son. He's eight months old, and he loves
everybody. Neatest kid in the world, although I

may be a little prejudiced. Honestly, though, he's no trouble at all. Can I pick you up around seven?"

"Uh—oh, sure," Chrissy stammered. "Seven will be just fine."

"Wonderful," Jim said. "Nancy's really looking forward to a night out together. She's been tied to the house so much since Joshua arrived." He got up and put his cup down on the tray. "Now I suppose we'd better get back to work. You two make sure the patients will be ready to go home, and I'll go face Miss Henshaw's poodle." He gave them both a big, friendly grin and went through to the front office.

Chrissy and Roger stood alone in the room. He gave her a long steady look before he picked up the tray and without a word walked through the doorway to the supply room.

He knows, Chrissy thought miserably. *He knows exactly what happened. Boy, have I ever made a fool of myself this time! What am I going to tell Cara? What am I going to tell the kids at school? How can I face anyone again?*

Chapter 9

The fact that Joshua Garrison turned out to be the world's sweetest baby and an absolute delight to sit for did little to make Chrissy feel better. She could not stop thinking about the stupid mistake she had made, and every time she thought about it, she went hot all over with embarrassment. She wished she had not bragged so much to Caroline and the kids at school. She wavered between telling them the truth and putting up with a lot of teasing or making up a convenient lie and feeling guilty about it.

She had kept up her pretense while both she and Caroline got ready for their "dates" on Friday evening. She had tried on several different outfits, settling in the end for a slim black skirt and long red shirt that made her look older than sixteen. She felt stupid and guilty, knowing that she was deceiving Caroline, but she couldn't find an appropriate moment to blurt out the truth. Caroline herself was excitedly dressing for her date to the Phil Collins concert with the fabulous drum player. So Chrissy let her cousin go on thinking that when Dr. Garrison honked the horn of his blue Volvo, he had come to pick her up for the date of her life.

When Caroline came home that night, Chrissy pretended to be asleep, and in the morning she was all ready with a smooth lie about the little French restaurant and how Dr. Garrison was friendly but not romantic. She would have carried it off, too, if she hadn't caught sight of her own reflection in the bedroom mirror. "You phony," it whispered back to her. "You can't deceive your own cousin and still like yourself."

"Go on, Chrissy," Caroline was saying. "You were about to tell me where you went on your date. Stop daydreaming!"

Chrissy turned to face her cousin. "It was all a big mistake, Cara," she said.

Caroline's eyes opened very wide. "You mean he came on strong?" she asked.

Chrissy shook her head in embarrassment. "Just the opposite. He wanted me to baby-sit his kid while he and his wife went out."

To Chrissy's horror, Caroline burst out laughing. "Oh, Chrissy, what a letdown!" she howled. "You left the house all dressed up, and he tricked you into baby-sitting. That could only happen to you!"

"He didn't trick me," Chrissy said angrily. "I found out it was baby-sitting. I just couldn't tell anyone because it made me look like a fool. I told you in the end because I thought you'd see my side of it, and I didn't like lying to you."

Caroline's smile faded, and she got up. "Oh, Chrissy, I am sorry," she said. "You must have been really disappointed. I'm really sorry. I won't laugh anymore."

Chrissy shrugged. "I guess it was funny when you think about it," she admitted. "The kids at school will laugh themselves silly when they hear about it. They'll all think I'm still a little hick who falls for anything. . . ."

"Then we won't tell them," Caroline said gently. "We'll say that it was just a friendly dinner to welcome a new employee. How about that?"

"That's what I was going to tell you," Chrissy said, "only I found that I couldn't lie to you."

Caroline smiled. "It's good to know we can tell each other everything—but the kids at school don't ever have to know."

On Monday, Caroline helped Chrissy get through the story smoothly. Dr. Garrison ended up sounding like a nice guy, and everyone agreed Chrissy was lucky to have a boss who took her out and didn't make a pass at her. But for the next few days, Chrissy made an effort to stay away from Roger. Every time she had to hurry past him in the hallway, he seemed to have the same mocking smile on his face—a smile that said all too clearly, "You were decent enough not to blab about me and the bucket, so I won't blab about you, but don't think I've forgotten!"

The closest he came to saying anything was on Monday afternoon. "So how did the baby-sit with Joshua go?" he asked.

"Very nice, thank you," she answered in a frosty voice, and fled from the room so fast that she caught her lab coat pocket on the doorknob.

Most of the time she didn't give him a chance to speak to her. If he came into a room, she found an instant excuse to inspect the kennels or get Jim a cup of coffee. At first Roger seemed surprised by her snubs, but then he became defensive, turning away when she came near or pointing out a job that she had left half-finished.

By the end of the week, Jim couldn't help noticing that something was wrong.

"Did you and Roger have a fight or something?" he asked Chrissy on Friday.

"No," she replied uneasily.

"Well, I definitely sense an atmosphere in this place, and I don't like it, Chrissy. Has he been bothering you?"

"No!" she said emphatically. The one thing she didn't want was for Roger to get into trouble because of her stupidity.

"And have you been bothering him?" Jim asked with a laugh.

"No!" she had to laugh, too. "I guess we just

don't have too much in common," she added.

"I was wondering whether Roger resented having you here, whether he wanted the job to himself and was making you feel unwelcome," Jim suggested. "He's very possessive about his animals, and he is a little overpowering in his enthusiasm at times, but he's a very nice boy."

"Oh, I know that," Chrissy said, "and he hasn't made me feel unwelcome, really."

"Then stop drifting around like two unfriendly ghosts," Jim said. "This place is beginning to give me the creeps."

"Okay," Chrissy said, pasting a fake smile on her face. After that, she made a big effort to be friendly to Roger when Jim was around but always found an excuse to leave the room the moment Jim did. She also noticed that Roger came in less on days when he was not scheduled, so she figured he wanted to avoid her, too.

Then one Wednesday afternoon, she came into the office to find Roger waiting for her, waving a piece of paper.

"Message from Jim," he muttered. "He had to go out on an emergency, and he'd promised to pick up an animal slated for surgery tomorrow. He's asked us both to do it for him."

He held the paper out to Chrissy. "The owner has unfortunately broken her leg," she read silently, "so I said we'd bring Godzilla in for her. I'm sure you two can manage it for me. It's only a couple of blocks away. Thanks—Jim.

"P.S. You might want to leave him in his traveling cage."

Chrissy gave Roger a quick glance. She noticed that his Adam's apple was moving up and down nervously.

"Do you think it needs two of us?" she asked, hoping he'd say no.

"Jim says both of us," Roger answered, his fair skin flushing as he spoke. "Besides, if it's a big cage . . ."

Chrissy was dying to find out if Roger knew what sort of animal Godzilla was, but she didn't want to admit that she might be scared.

"Godzilla!" she said with an attempt at a light laugh. "The dumb names people call their pets."

"Right!" Roger said with a similar laugh. "Are you ready, then?"

"Sure I'm ready. Let's go," Chrissy said, walking ahead of him out the front door. She glanced at the paper again. "This is someone's address, isn't it?"

"What do you mean?"

"I mean, it's not the zoo? I mean, I wouldn't want to stagger all the way from the zoo with an animal in a cage."

Roger looked at her scornfully. "Jim wouldn't expect us to walk all the way from the zoo," he said. "Besides, the zoo has its own vet."

Chrissy heaved a small sigh of relief. At least it was a pet animal, and she wouldn't be crossing San Francisco with a leopard or a gorilla grabbing at her face all the way. People weren't allowed to keep dangerous animals as pets, were they? And yet the cage was heavy enough to require two people. . . . Chrissy was almost dying of curiosity.

"Roger, what do you think—" she began, exactly at the same moment as she said: "I wonder what—"

They both stopped and giggled self-consciously.

"Go on," Chrissy said politely.

"No, you first," he said gallantly.

"I was just wondering what sort of animal it might be," Chrissy said.

Roger grinned as if he had scored a point. "Having second thoughts?" he asked. "I hope you're not going to turn chicken and run out on me?"

"You don't want to face it alone?"

"Not that—I might not be able to carry a large cage by myself."

"Oh."

They walked along in silence.

"Forty-six is over there," Roger said. "It's an apartment block. Well, one thing, you can't keep anything too exotic in an apartment."

"You're just as scared as me about what this animal is," Chrissy said with a triumphant laugh.

"I am not scared," Roger said. "I'm just curious. I mean, if it was a large alligator or something . . ."

"An alligator?" Chrissy hadn't considered that possibility. She imagined her fingers being eaten off, one by one, as she held the cage.

"People do keep alligators!" Roger commented.

"If it's an alligator, you carry it," Chrissy said firmly.

"I thought you said you weren't scared."

"I just happen to like my fingers," Chrissy said. "I need all of them to pick up a slice of pizza."

For the first time Roger looked directly at her and grinned. "I bet it turns out to be a hamster," he said.

When they reached the apartment, a gentle-looking elderly lady opened the door. "Oh, you're from Dr. Garrison's office. How kind," she said. "Emma Hatfield. Do come in. I'm so grateful. As you can see"—she pointed down to the cast on her foot—"I can't go out at the moment, and poor old Godzilla has to have the nasty cyst removed from his hand. It hurts him to climb." She waved graciously at a velvet-covered sofa. "Please take a seat. I'll go and make sure he's ready for his big adventure."

As soon as she left the room Roger and Chrissy turned to each other. Roger shrugged and began tapping his foot. *How can he be so cool?* Chrissy wondered. *This animal has a cyst on his hand and can't climb—it must be a gorilla!*

Chrissy sat very still on the sofa, trying to ignore the noises from the next room, where it sounded as if something large were leaping around. "Now come down at once," Miss Hatfield said, her voice sounding strained. "I know you don't like the nasty cage, but you have to go in it." She raised her voice to call through to Roger and Chrissy. "Poor Godzilla's not in a very good mood today. You will be careful with him, won't you?"

"Yes, ma'am," Roger called back with an amused glance at Chrissy, but she noticed now that he was tapping his foot twice as fast.

Miss Hatfield went on in a soothing voice, "Down you come. Down to Mama." Next followed the sound of scuffling, the clunk of Miss Hatfield's cast, something falling over and breaking. "Bad boy!" Miss Hatfield's voice was no longer soothing. "Look what you've done! It's no good hiding on top of the curtains. I can still see you. Now, down you come, whether you like it or not!" More scuffling, more breaking sounds, and then the most terrifying high-pitched screams. Chrissy clutched the arm of the sofa and wondered if she should try to make an escape before it was too late.

A few moments later Miss Hatfield appeared again, breathing heavily and with her neat gray hair in disarray. "There," she said. "The naughty boy didn't want to come down from the curtains, but he knows he has to obey. He's quite ready for you now—do you want to come through and get him?"

She led the way into another room that was luxuriously decorated but showed clear evidence of the scuffle that had just taken place. On a table in the middle of the room was a small cage, and in the cage was a tiny black-faced monkey, no bigger than a toy, holding on to the bars and screeching with rage.

"Now, Godzilla, stop that horrible noise," Miss Hatfield said. "These nice young people are going to take you to make your hand feel better. Be gentle with him, won't you, he's so delicate!" She picked up a tartan blanket from a chair. "And we must keep the cage covered. He catches cold so easily." She covered him tenderly, but the blanket only slightly muffled his screams.

Chrissy didn't dare look in Roger's direction as they carried the cage, the monkey still screaming inside it, down the steps and out into the street. It was only when they were well clear of the building that they looked at each other and burst out laughing.

"And you were worried about meeting an alligator!" Roger teased.

"I was not," Chrissy retorted. "I was worried about it being a gorilla, if you must know."

"Well, it's only one step away from a gorilla, so you were close!" Roger said, laughing. "And he's making enough noise for a whole family of gorillas."

Godzilla kept up his screams all the way to the office, causing Roger to become very embarrassed whenever anyone turned to look at them. Chrissy, on the other hand, was finding the whole thing very funny, as she hurried to keep up with Roger's rapid pace.

They finally brought the monkey in through the back door and set him down in the hallway.

When they took off his blanket, he stopped screaming and looked at them imploringly, reaching out his tiny hands through the bars toward them.

"You sweet little thing," Chrissy cooed, holding out her finger to him. "You're not so vicious, are you?" The next minute she yelped, "Ow, he just bit me! Did you see that?"

"Now you know why he's named after a monster," Roger said. "Where should we leave him, do you think?"

"On the table in the supply room?" Chrissy asked. "It's warm in there and far enough away to muffle his screams if he starts again."

Roger was squatting down, making friends with the little animal. "I hate to see him spend the night in a cage as small as this," he said. "Couldn't we find somewhere else to put him?"

"He'd slip right through the bars of the cages here," Chrissy said. "They were designed for dogs."

"We have a big cat cage out back," Roger suggested. "I could go and get that. It has mesh over the front. At least he could move around more in that until his operation."

"I don't think that's a good idea, Roger," Chrissy said. "He's safe where he is."

"But he hardly has room to turn around. That's just a carrying cage. I'll find the cat cage, okay?" And he went without waiting for her answer, returning a few minutes later with a spacious wire-fronted box. "See—this is much nicer. We'll put him in here." Before Chrissy could stop him, he opened the front of the cage to lift the little monkey out. But Godzilla was too quick. He slipped free and bounded down from the table.

"Oh, no," Roger cried. "Catch him, before he gets—" The sentence was never finished as the monkey leaped toward the door and squeezed around it. Chrissy and Roger gave each other a horrified glance, then rushed after the monkey.

"We don't want to scare him," Roger cautioned as they opened the door onto the hall.

"Scare him?" Chrissy demanded. "More likely he'll scare the daylights out of anyone who sees him."

Godzilla was already having a great time, swinging from bar to bar down the row of cages, just above the heads of the dogs inside them. The dogs were going crazy, barking and leaping at the creature above their heads. Chrissy and Roger ran after the monkey, yelling instructions at each other all the way down the hallway. "Grab him!" "No, you grab him! Quick, as he swings past the setter."

"No, right now—oh, you missed him!"

"He's over there!"

Finally the monkey paused for breath at the top of the last cage. "Now I've got him cornered," Roger called triumphantly. He moved a stool underneath the monkey and slowly reached out. Just as he made a grab, Godzilla leaped across the hallway to catch the door frame opposite.

The stool with Roger on it teetered and came crashing to the ground.

"Are you all right?" Chrissy asked, hauling him to his feet.

He nodded grimly. "If he goes anywhere near Annie, I'm in big trouble," he said, rubbing his elbow as he stood up.

The monkey had taken the shortcut to the front office, by way of the consulting room. Luckily the consulting room was empty as Godzilla bounced on the examination table, waving a pair of forceps in his hand as if it were a trophy.

"Drop those right now and come here," Chrissy said in her most commanding voice. The monkey appeared to cower and let the instrument fall. "I've got him," Chrissy whispered, reaching out behind his back. Then, at the last moment, the monkey dodged her hand, danced along the table, knocking everything flying as he leaped down from it, and scampered out into the front hall. Only a few more yards, and he would reach the waiting room and Annie's desk. Chrissy could already see Annie's neat gray hair as she sat with her back to them. She could also see several patients in the waiting room, including a woman with a cat box sitting close to the door. The monkey slowed down as he approached the room full of people. He sat in the doorway, as if thinking over what to do next, while Chrissy and Roger sneaked up behind him.

Godzilla was staring hard at Annie as if fascinated by her gray bun. Chrissy could almost see his little mind working, calculating the size of leap needed to land on Annie's back. Chrissy and Roger both knelt down and crept toward him, four hands ready to grab. The monkey must have heard the noise behind him because he started to look around. As he turned his head he found himself staring straight at the huge tom cat in the box near the door. The cat obviously didn't think too much of Godzilla, because it stood up, arching its back and raising its fur. Then the cat gave a loud, menacing meow. Godzilla leaped straight into the air in fright and turned to run away. At the same time Chrissy and Roger each closed a hand around him. they struggled to their feet, still both clasping the monkey.

Annie swiveled around at the noise. "What's going on?" she asked.

"Er, nothing Annie. Sorry about the noise," Chrissy said, poking her head around the doorway and trying to keep a straight face.

"Well, get back to work, and keep it down back there," Annie snapped.

Roger and Chrissy hurried together with the monkey back to the supply room and stuffed him, complaining loudly, into his own cage. It was only when the door was finally shut that they both heaved sighs of relief.

"Thanks," Roger said.

"For what?"

"For not giving me away. I was the one who let the monkey out, after all. You could have let everyone know how dumb I was."

"Why would I want to do that?"

"Well, I thought you didn't like me very much," Roger said, looking down at the floor. "I got the impression you thought I was a real dumb klutz and too far beneath you to even talk to me."

"Only because you were enjoying the joke on me."

"What joke?"

"You know, about last Friday—missing out on the Phil Collins concert to baby-sit."

"How come that's a joke?" he asked. "I thought you'd already committed yourself to the baby-sit—that was why you turned down the concert. At least, I hoped it was that. I hoped it wasn't that you'd rather baby-sit than be seen out with me."

"Oh, no," Chrissy said. "You see I thought that you thought that . . ."

"Thought what?"

"Oh, never mind," Chrissy said hastily.

"You know what I thought?" Roger went on softly. "I thought you must be a really nice person because you didn't want to let Jim down. I also thought you must be nice because you didn't tell him about my little episode with the bucket."

"Oh." For once Chrissy was lost for words. She was overwhelmed by the feelings of guilt and embarrassment and relief that were flooding through her.

"I guess you must think I'm a permanent klutz after today," Roger said after a long silence. "Letting the monkey out and then falling off the stool. What a disaster."

"It wasn't a disaster. In fact, it was kind of fun!" Chrissy said.

"You thought so?"

"Sure I did. A disaster would have been if he'd landed on Annie's head!" Their eyes met for a moment.

Roger started to laugh. "It might have been kind of interesting, though."

Chrissy nodded. "You know, it might almost have been worth it, to watch her expression."

They stood laughing together.

"Listen," Roger said at last, "I don't suppose you'd like to go have some pizza with me, when we get off work?" His eyes looked at her pleadingly, although his voice was casual. "To celebrate not losing any fingers?"

Chrissy looked down at her scratched and bitten hands, then grinned up at Roger. "Sure," she said. "I'd like that."

Chapter 10

"So when do I get to meet Jeff?" Chrissy asked Caroline.

They were sitting together in Mama's Ice Cream Parlor on their afternoon off. Now that they both had money again, they'd ordered their favorite Cable Car sundaes.

Caroline made a face. "I don't know if I'll let you meet him ever," she said.

"Meaning what?"

"Meaning that I know you, Chrissy Madden. You'll start flirting with him instantly, and before I know it, you'll have lured him away."

Chrissy grinned broadly. "So you are getting interested in him after all?" she asked. "All that pretending he meant nothing to you was just bluff!"

Caroline toyed with her napkin. "I don't know whether I feel anything for him or not," she said. "It's early days yet. We've only been out together twice, and in the store we're too busy to talk most of the time. He's a nice guy." She shrugged her shoulders. "Apart from that, we'll just have to see . . . but I won't even have a chance if you start fluttering those gorgeous eyelashes in his direction."

"You make me sound like a femme fatale!" Chrissy giggled. "See what impressive words I'm picking up here? If I used words like that on Ben, he'd only say, 'What're you talking about, girl?' "

Caroline scooped up another spoonful of ice cream. "Poor old Ben," she said. "Coming here was destined to change you."

"I know," Chrissy agreed. "But maybe it was a good thing, Cara. After all, I don't want to think about settling down for many, many years yet, and Ben was all for talking about getting married as soon as we graduate. That would never have worked. Can you see me as a housewife?"

Caroline laughed. "Frankly, no," she said. "You can't even eat your sundae without making a mess."

Chrissy looked in front of her and wiped up the puddle of hot fudge on the table. "You're just changing the subject because you don't want me to meet Jeff," Chrissy said. "I'll start creeping down to the store and spying on you soon."

"You'd better not," Caroline said. "Knowing

you, you'd probably knock over a drum set worth a few thousand."

"I would not! You make me sound as bad as Roger."

"He can't be too bad," Caroline said, "or you'd never have gone out for pizza with him last week. Or was the pizza only out of pity?"

"No, of course it wasn't," Chrissy said, then stopped, thinking over what she had just said. She'd had fun with Roger that night—she found that she could really talk to him about interesting things. She didn't have to pretend to be a culture vulture, as she had done when she'd gone out with Hunter Bryce. Roger's one consuming interest was animals. He had visited farms and wanted to know more about horses and cows and pigs. She could tell him funny stories about her pet piglet and the time she hid it in the washing basket, or the time they kept a goat that ate the legs off all the long johns. She had learned to clam up about stories like that around the kids at school. She noticed that they gave her odd looks and glanced at each other in amusement when they thought she wasn't looking. But Roger hadn't thought her stories were weird at all. Talking to him had reminded her of regular dinner table conversation back home. In fact, once during the evening she had just stopped herself in time from calling him Ben!

"Roger is a nice guy," she added.

Caroline nodded. "And when am I going to meet the fabulous Roger?" she asked. "Do I have to come down to the vet's office and spy on you?"

Chrissy giggled. "If you'd come down yesterday, you'd have been able to watch Roger's latest disaster! He locked himself into a kennel."

Caroline's eyes lit up with amusement. "On purpose?" she giggled.

"No, just another Roger accident. He was in there cleaning it, and he'd left the back door open to get air when the wind swung the door shut with him inside. Luckily I arrived to rescue him, or he'd've had to spend the night with a German shepherd and two spaniels!"

"Poor guy, he does sound as if he needs someone to watch out for him," Caroline said. "I'm glad you're taking on the job. I think it's very noble of you."

"It's a sacrifice," Chrissy said, "but someone has to do it."

She went back to attacking her hot-fudge sundae, feeling uneasy when she realized how she had put Roger down again. After all, the guy wasn't that much of a klutz. It was just that weird things seemed to happen to him sometimes. *I should be more understanding*, she decided, *because things like that happen to me, too.*

It was almost dark when they finished their sundaes and came out into the street. "You go on," Chrissy told Caroline. "I've got to pop into the vet's office. I think I left my hairbrush in the bathroom."

"You think I can't see through that lame excuse?" Caroline laughed. "You just want a chance to go see Roger."

"He'll have gone home long ago," Chrissy said.

"Unless he's locked himself in another kennel," Caroline said with a grin.

Chrissy winced. Why had she given Caroline completely the wrong impression about him. *Caroline must think that Roger's a complete nerd now*, she thought, *when he's really just a nice, ordinary boy who sometimes gets into a pickle.*

"I'll see you in a while," she said, stopping at the corner.

"You want me to come with you?"

"No, don't bother. I'll catch up with you probably before you get home."

"Okay," Caroline said. "I still think it's a secret meeting you don't want me in on. I bet this Roger is really a total babe, and you're just saying all this stuff to keep us fooled." She laughed and turned up the hill toward their apartment, while Chrissy continued along the street to the office.

She let herself through the gate into the small side yard and walked around to the back door. There wasn't a light on in the whole building. So Jim didn't have any last-minute emergencies for once! She opened the back door and walked in, switching on the hall light. As she passed on of the cages along the hallway, she saw something move, and it certainly wasn't a dog or cat. Chrissy let out a little scream and jumped back.

"It's only me," Roger said, looking up at Chrissy from his position on the floor. "Sorry if I scared you. What are you doing here?"

"Holy cow! Are you determined to give me heart failure?" Chrissy yelled. "What am I doing here? Haven't we had this conversation before? If you really want to know, I left my brush in the bathroom. So the big question is: What are you doing here? It's seven o'clock, for Pete's sake. Did you get shut in a cage again?"

"Not exactly," Roger said. "I decided to stay and keep an eye on Trapper."

"On what?"

Roger motioned to the dog at the back of the cage behind him. A large golden labrador lay stretched out, sound asleep. "He got hit by a car today," Roger said. "Jim tried to stitch him up, but he's hurt pretty bad. I didn't want to leave him alone all night, in case he woke up from the anesthetic and got scared. He's such a beautiful dog . . . ."

He went over and knelt down beside the still body, gently running his fingers over the silky back. Chrissy looked slowly from the dog to Roger's enthusiastic face. "So you're going to sit here all night?" she asked.

Roger nodded. "I don't mind," he said. "I wouldn't want him to damage his broken leg or bust his stitches."

"What did Jim say?"

"Jim said he should sleep until morning," Roger admitted, "but you never know with animals. Some come out of the anesthetic much quicker than others."

Chrissy squatted down beside the dog. It reminded her of Bonnie, her dog back in Danbury. If Bonnie ever got hurt, she would certainly stay with her all night, but for Roger to do it for a dog that wasn't even his—well, that was really something. "You really care about animals, don't you?" she asked uncertainly.

Roger nodded. "More than anything," he said. "Animals are so noble. They don't make a fuss when they are suffering. They love you and don't ask anything in return. They don't put you down if you're not the world's greatest football player."

"Who does that?" Chrissy asked.

"My dad," Roger said, turning his head to look at the sleeping dog. "My dad happens to be a football coach, and I am the world's biggest disappointment to him. I always have been."

"But you can't help it if you're not good at football," Chrissy said. "You're not built for it. You're too skinny."

"My dad thinks that it's my fault I'm skinny," Roger said with a slight grin. "He thinks I don't eat enough just to spite him."

"Poor old Roger," Chrissy said, patting his arm fondly.

Roger drew his arm away as if she had burned him. "That's another thing," he said in a tight voice. "People always feel sorry for me. Do you have any idea what it does to your ego if people are always saying, 'Poor old Roger, and he's such a klutz.' That's another reason I like animals. They don't judge you. As long as you're nice to them, they think you're perfect."

"Hey, I wasn't putting you down," Chrissy said. "I really like you."

"Really?" Roger asked, his eyes opening wide.

"I've been out for pizza with you, haven't I? I'm a pretty choosy person. I wouldn't be seen out with just anybody, you know."

Roger turned his attention back to the dog. "I suspect that's more because you feel sorry for me than that you are madly attracted to me."

"I can tell who feels sorry for you," Chrissy exploded. "You do! If you go through life saying 'Poor little me' and expecting everybody to be down on you, then they will be. You have a lot going for you, Roger."

"Like what?"

"You're tall. You could be good-looking if only you didn't wear those old sweatshirts all the time and you did something with your hair. And most important of all, you are a very nice person. I really admire you for staying all night with a dog you don't even know. It takes a really nice person to do that."

"You're not just saying that?" Roger said hesitantly.

"I don't just say things," Chrissy objected. "When you get to know me better, you'll know that one of my faults is that I say just what I think. I did feel sorry for you when we first met, but now I know there is nothing to feel sorry about."

Roger looked across at her, holding her eyes

with his. "Does that mean you'd go to another concert with me if I asked you?" he said quietly.

Chrissy nodded. "I'd like to go to a concert with you, Roger," she said.

Roger's eyes twinkled behind his glasses. Chrissy noticed for the first time how big and brown his eyes were. "What sort of music do you like best?" he asked.

"Anything except the real hard rock, heavy metal stuff. I don't like people who spit at you and break their guitars."

Roger laughed. "Me neither. There's a local group I think are very good. They're called The Earthquakes, and they do a lot of sixties stuff— you know, Beatles and early Stones."

"I love Beatles music," Chrissy said excitedly.

Roger's face lit up. "You want to go, then?"

"You bet!" Chrissy said, rising slowly to her feet. "I'm really looking forward to it, Roger, but right now I ought to be going. My cousin will wonder what happened to me." She looked back at Roger, still kneeling protectively beside the dog. "Will you be okay here? Do you have something to eat?"

"I'll be fine," he said. "I've come well prepared. Sleeping bag and all."

Still she hesitated. "I could come back later, after dinner, and sit with you for a while," she offered.

He looked embarrassed. "You don't have to do that," he said.

"I wouldn't mind. I could bring my homework.

I bet you're good at math, aren't you?"

"Pretty good."

"See—I knew it. You can help me with my math homework."

"Oh, if you're only coming to get help with math, that's okay."

Chrissy glared at him. "Don't start on that again, or I won't come," she said. "I'm coming because I don't like to think of you all alone here, and I want to keep you company. Okay?"

"Well, if you're sure!"

"Roger! I'll hit you over the head in a moment!" Chrissy said, laughing. "I am sure. I'll see you in about an hour. Any requests for snacks?"

"No, that's okay. Well, maybe some chips. Sour cream and onion, if possible. And a candy bar— or how about a box of Cracker Jacks?"

"Nothing else, sir?" Chrissy asked sarcastically. "How about a portable TV or a hot tub?"

"Get out of here!" he said, grinning at her.

She smiled back. "That's better," she said. "I'm going to work on you, Roger. All you need is a large dose of self-confidence. By the time I've finished, you won't know yourself!"

Chapter 11

The band played out the last notes of the tune. "Thank you, thank you," the lead singer breathed into the microphone. "We're going to take a short break now, then we'll be back with more music."

Roger turned to Chrissy. "Enjoying it?" he asked. He looked at her shyly, his brown eyes twinkling hopefully behind his glasses. Chrissy noticed that he had taken a lot of trouble to dress well for the concert. He was not wearing one of his ancient sweatshirts, but a pale yellow crew-neck sweater with black jeans, which made him look tall and elegant. Nobody would think that this was the sort of person who walked around with buckets on his feet.

She smiled at him and nodded. "It's really great, Rog. This group is good."

"Of course this isn't exactly as impressive as concerts at the Oakland Colliseum," Roger said.

"Are you kidding?" Chrissy countered. "This is the first concert I've been to since I got here, and the only concerts I've been to back in Iowa were in rinky-dink little theaters. I did drive all the way to Omaha once to see Sting, but they had so many security guards and police standing around, it was more like a police convention than a concert."

Roger laughed. "I'd really like to see your farm sometime," he said. "I've never had much chance to study farm animals."

"Well, you'd have too good a chance where I live," Chrissy said. "What with our dairy cows, and the horses and the neighbor's pigs, we spend our lives around farm animals."

"Hey, that's great," Roger said. "Do you think I might go and help out one summer? That would be fabulous experience for me."

"I don't see why not," Chrissy said.

"Oh, wow," Roger replied eagerly. "You really think they'd let me?"

Chrissy laughed. "My brothers would be delighted to have you do their chores," she said. "And if you'd get up and milk at five o'clock every morning, my dad would love you forever, too."

"And what could I do for you to make you love me forever?" Roger asked lightly. He flushed immediately after he had said it.

Chrissy laughed uneasily. "I'll have to think

about that one," she said, "but I can talk to my folks for you and ask them about helping out."

"I think that would be just great, Chrissy," Roger said.

"You think you'd like to be a country vet someday?"

Roger looked down. "What I'd really like to do," he began in a quiet voice, "is to work with marine mammals. I'm especially interested in dolphins and whales. Do you know that dolphins have superior brain power to human beings, and that whales have a remarkable ability to recover from wounds that would mean certain death to humans?"

Chrissy shook her head politely.

"I've read a lot about marine mammals, and I've also been helping out with the sea lions at the Marine Mammal Center. But I don't think I'll ever get a job like that—there are only one or two veterinarians in the country who are marine mammal experts."

"So why not you?" Chrissy asked.

Roger looked embarrassed. "I don't really think I'll be at the top of the class of graduating vets," he said. "With my grades, I'll just scrape into graduate school if I'm lucky. I guess I'll be happy to settle for dogs and cats, and maybe a few cows and horses."

"That sounds okay," Chrissy said. "A small-town vet, treating some farm animals and some pets, living in a house with a white picket fence in a town where everyone knows your name. . . ."

"Exactly," said Roger. "That's exactly what I want." They looked at each other for a moment. "And what do you want?" Roger asked her.

Chrissy shrugged. "I don't even know," she said. "I thought once I wanted to be a vet, too, but I don't think I'll ever get the grades in math and chemistry to be able to consider it. I don't even know if I'd be tough enough to be a vet. I'd get really upset if any of the animals died."

"A farmer's daughter?" Roger asked in amazement. "I would have thought you'd be used to it."

Chrissy shook her head. "Not me," she said. "I'm a joke in my family. I always had to leave when Dad killed a chicken or when the next-door neighbors killed a pig. I was just born soft-hearted."

"I like that," Roger said. "I know I'm soft-hearted, too, but I don't mind the thought of operating on animals."

"I bet you'll make a terrific vet," Chrissy said. "I think it's really important to care, as well as being a good doctor."

Roger's eyes held hers. "You know, Chrissy, I feel like I can really talk to you. I've never dared to tell anyone else about my dreams," he said quietly, "but I can tell you understand, and you don't think I'm stupid."

"Of course I don't think you're stupid. Your dreams sound pretty good to me. Much better than being stuck in a noisy, polluted city and rushing to an office from nine to five!"

Roger smiled happily. "It's amazing how much

we have in common," he remarked.

They sat in a comfortable silence then, until people began to drift back to their seats after the break.

"I can't get over the way kids dress here," Chrissy commented. "And the hairstyles! Look at that girl with the half-shaved, half-blue head."

"Interesting," Roger said. "Maybe I should consider something like that for me, now that I've been told to upgrade my image!"

"Roger!" Chrissy shrieked in horror.

His eyes twinkled. "Just kidding," he said. "Can you imagine my dad, the football coach, if I came home with blue spiked hair?"

"Worse than that, the dogs would start growling at you," Chrissy said, giggling. She felt relaxed and content. It was fun to laugh and joke with Roger. He was so different from her friends at Maxwell, who always tried to act a certain way. Roger was just plain Roger, and she liked that.

"It might be worth it," Roger mused, "to see Annie's face if I came into the office with a shaved head or spiked hair. Add a leather jacket to that and a few bits of chain, and she wouldn't dare order me around anymore."

"Keep your voice down," Chrissy whispered. "There's a guy dressed just like that sitting two seats away from us—and the chains don't look as if they're for show, either."

Roger stole a glance. "Half this audience looks as if it escaped from San Quentin," he said.

"I hope you're not putting us in that half,"

Chrissy commented dryly. "Actually, when you look around, there are plenty of sharp dressers here, too. Some people look really great—that guy in the turquoise shirt and . . . holy cow, that's Cara!"

"That's what?" Roger asked.

"My cousin. The one I live with. That's her, and that guy must be Jeff! I didn't know they'd be here tonight."

Chrissy watched in astonishment as Caroline and Jeff stepped past the people in their row to get back to their seats. When Caroline had described Jeff as a cute guy, that had been the understatement of the century! His blond-streaked hair was cut in a surfer style, very short at the sides and flopping across his forehead. His tan accentuated the blond hair and the bright blue shirt and the tight white jeans. Chrissy could not take her eyes off him. *Wow*, she thought, *no wonder Cara's been keeping him well away from me.*

"Maybe we should go down and say hi," she suggested to Roger.

"But the intermission is almost over," Roger said hesitantly.

"You keep our seats, then, and I'll pop down," Chrissy said. "I'll just be a minute."

Without waiting for him to say anything further, she pushed her way past the members of the chain gang in the seats beside her and hurried down the aisle. The band was already up on stage, checking the plugs on the amps and warming up. Chrissy fought past the crush of people in the aisles.

"You can't get down here, it's already too full," one girl complained as Chrissy squished past.

"Cara!" Chrissy yelled.

Caroline turned toward the call. "Chrissy! What are you doing here?" she asked.

At last Chrissy made her way over to her cousin. "I'm here with Roger," she said. "Remember I told you he had tickets for a concert this weekend?"

"Oh, Roger!" Caroline looked relieved. "Where is he?"

"Saving our seats," Chrissy said. "I just caught a glimpse of you, and I had to come down and say hi!" She beamed at Caroline, and her gaze strayed to the gorgeous boy beside her. He smiled as her eyes met his, and his smile was so terrific that her knees almost melted. But not a bit like Luke, she thought. How could Cara have thought so?

"Uh, you must be Jeff," Chrissy managed to stammer. "I've heard so much about you."

"That's right—Jeff Dixon. And you are . . . ?" Jeff asked politely.

"I'm Chrissy."

A big grin spread across Jeff's face. "The crazy cousin, huh?"

Chrissy noted Caroline's embarrassed look, but she wasn't embarrassed at all. "Yeah, pretty crazy, I guess," she said. "Crazy people have more fun."

Jeff smiled as if he understood. "Cara's told me
a lot about you," he said. As he spoke he idly
slipped an arm around Caroline's shoulder—a
gesture that sent a pang of jealousy through
Chrissy. *Cool it, Chrissy*, she warned herself.
Remember, he's Caroline's boyfriend. She managed to keep on smiling. "I hope it wasn't all
bad?" she asked.

Caroline shifted uneasily. "Of course it wasn't,"
she said. "So, where's Roger?"

"He's way up there. Look—up where that exit
sign is. That row. See the guys with the punk
haircuts?"

"Roger's got a punk haircut?"

"No, dummy. See the empty seat beside that
group? Next to that."

"I only see a guy in a yellow sweater."

"That's him."

"But he looks good, Chrissy. I was expecting a
total nerd from your description. He looks really
cool!"

"He does tonight, I'll agree," Chrissy said. "I've
been working on his image a little."

The lights in the auditorium began to dim. The
lead singer came to the front of the stage, picked
up his microphone, and began blowing into it
experimentally.

"You'd better get back to your seat, or you'll
never find it again," Caroline said, giving Chrissy
a gentle push.

"Okay. See you guys later, maybe," Chrissy said.
As she looked back to wave, she added impul-

sively, "Why don't we meet after the concert for a bite to eat?"

"Yeah, good idea," Jeff agreed. "Shall we meet them by the box office in the front, Cara?"

"Okay," Caroline said, but her next words were drowned out by the lead singer.

"Welcome back, everybody!" he yelled.

Amidst a chorus of cheers and whistles, Chrissy hurried to make her seat before she got trapped in the aisle. She could see Roger's glasses reflecting back the light from the stage. He was looking anxiously in her direction, like a little kid in a supermarket who'd lost his mother.

At that moment the auditorium was plunged into darkness . . . and the band broke into a loud, earth-shaking number. Chrissy groped for what she hoped was her row of seats. Instead her hand touched the bearded face of a member of the chain gang. "Hey, watch it," he growled.

"Sorry, I'm just trying to get back to my seat," she murmured.

"That's okay, doll-face, you can sit right here," he grunted, trying to pull her onto his knee.

"Thanks, but I already have a seat," she said, fighting his grasp. "It's right next to my boyfriend, the Sumo wrestler."

With that she wrenched herself free and stumbled past the other punkers down the row.

"You only just made it," Roger whispered as she sank onto the seat beside him. "I thought I'd lost you for a moment there." His face almost brushed hers as he whispered, and for a moment he rested his hand on top of hers. Chrissy didn't move. She didn't want to encourage Roger—especially when her heart was still pounding at the thought of the boy she had just met.

Poor old Rog, Chrissy thought with a sigh. *You might have lost me back there! Too bad Jeff Dixon happens to be dating my cousin!*

Chapter 12

"So did everyone enjoy the concert?" Chrissy asked brightly as they all sat at the cafe a few hours later.

Roger said, "Great," as the same time as Jeff said, "Pretty good."

There was another silence. At the back of the cafe a jukebox was blaring out a soulful Mexican number. Apart from three men at a back table, they were the only people there.

"I wish they'd hurry up with the hot chocolate," Roger said. They all looked around, but no one said anything.

"So how did you and Chrissy meet, Roger," Jeff asked at last. He smiled amiably at both Roger and Chrissy, but Chrissy glanced away quickly. Why did he have to be so darn good-looking?

Why did he have to have that wonderful smile? And worst of all, why did he have to be dating her cousin?

"We met at the veterinarian's office where we both work," Roger said, and Chrissy could sense his uneasiness. Roger gave a nervous cough in the back of his throat. "But I think you could say that we really met when we both had to chase a monkey!"

"Chase a monkey?"

Jeff and Cara both looked amused. Chrissy flushed. Why did he have to bring that up here? It made them both look weird, didn't it?

"Hey, that's really unique," Jeff said, grinning broadly. "If you two get married one day, you can go on the *Newlywed Game*. I can just hear you now—'That's right, Bob, we met while chasing a monkey.' 'Hey, good story, Roger and Chrissy. How about that, folks!'" Chrissy thought that Jeff's imitation was very funny, but she could tell that Roger wasn't amused.

"So didn't you two meet knocking over a double bass or something?" Chrissy said, trying hard to switch the conversation around.

"Nothing like that," Jeff said, looking fondly at Caroline. "Caroline showed up one afternoon, and Mr. Simon asked me to show her where everything was. I couldn't believe my luck." He casually put his arm around Caroline, while Chrissy glanced away and pretended to look for the waitress.

"We had to stack this music," Caroline added,

"and I blurted out, 'Oh, look, Gustav Holst's "The Planets." I love that,' and Jeff said, 'Hey, we just played that with the Youth Orchestra.' I was really surprised to find he was with the Youth Orchestra, because my parents are friends with the conductor. So after that we found that we knew lots of people in common."

You hear that, Chrissy Madden! Chrissy said firmly to herself. *Cara and Jeff have everything in common, just like you and Roger. So don't go stirring things up.* The hot chocolates arrived then, banged down ungraciously on the table by a surly waitress. Chrissy glanced at Jeff's amused face as the cream spilled onto the table in front of him. *If only he weren't so gorgeous,* she thought with a big sigh. *If only my heart didn't turn somersaults every time he smiled. Roger just doesn't do that to me.*

She looked over to Roger and found that he had been watching her.

He smiled at her shyly. *Oh geez, I hope he didn't catch me staring at Jeff,* she thought guiltily. *I've got to forget about Jeff—he belongs to Cara. Besides, it's Roger who's the right boy for me.*

Chrissy felt comfortable with Roger, and he seemed to understand how she felt lots of times. Even when she blurted out something about the farm back home that would have cracked up the other kids, Roger found it interesting. In fact, he seemed almost like a brother. Chrissy paused with this last thought. *Maybe that's the problem,*

she decided. *Roger gives me a feeling of security,
like having one of my brothers around, but I just
don't think of him in a romantic way. Boy, have I
got myself in a mess. I can't hurt Roger, and I
certainly can't hurt Cara. Jeff probably won't
even think about me after tonight, anyway. Darn,
I wish I'd never met him.*

The waitress shuffled back with a check.
"We're closing in five minutes," she said in a
growl. "You'd better drink up fast."

The four of them exchanged amused glances.

"I like the atmosphere in this place," Jeff said
smoothly, and Chrissy couldn't help gazing into
his wonderful laughing eyes. "There's something
about it—elegant yet dignified, restful yet stimu-
lating . . ." His description was interrupted by a
loud crash. Everyone turned around to see a
stack of chairs lying on the floor.

The four of them burst out laughing, fished out
their money, and got up to leave.

"I think I can safely say that was one of the
more forgettable restaurants I've ever visited,"
Jeff commented as they came out into the crisp
night air. He slipped his hand into Caroline's and
the two couples turned in opposite directions.

Chrissy and Roger were silent as they walked
to Roger's old car and climbed in. Neither of
them said anything on the way home, either, but
each time Roger looked at her with his big brown
eyes, she found herself thinking of Jeff's laughing
blue ones.

What is the matter with me? she asked herself

bleakly. *All the time I've been in San Francisco, I've longed for someone who liked me for what I am, who understood about the things that are important to me. And now that I've found a boy like that, I can't stop thinking about another boy who is totally unsuitable for me and who is obviously crazy about my cousin. I've got to stop thinking about him right now!*

With tremendous willpower she shut the laughing eyes out of her mind and snuggled closer to Roger. They drew up outside her block, and Roger turned off the engine. She turned and smiled at him.

"Thanks for the great evening," she said warmly.

"Thank you for coming with me," Roger answered.

"I really enjoyed myself, Rog," she insisted. And it was true: she had enjoyed being with Roger, laughing together at the weird people, telling him stories about her life back home, listening to his stories about the animals. In fact, if she hadn't caught sight of a turquoise shirt halfway through the concert, it would have been one of the nicest evenings she'd had since she arrived in California.

She sensed then that he was sliding his arm around the back of the seat, and she knew that meant he would probably try and kiss her. For a moment she thought of making a graceful getaway, but she decided to stay where she was as he moved gently toward her.

"I've *really* enjoyed tonight, Chrissy," he murmured in a low voice. "I still can't believe that a girl like you would . . ."

He was very close to her now, and she could see the apprehension in his eyes. *He's such a nice guy*, she thought for at least the hundredth time that night. *One little kiss won't hurt.*

"Yes, Roger?" she asked as if she were speaking her lines in a play.

"I mean, you are so pretty and—"

"Roger?" she interrupted.

"Yes?"

"Why don't you go ahead and kiss me?"

"Really?"

"Really."

"Wow, Chrissy," he said, and brought his lips toward hers. His kiss was hesitant at first, but not as clumsy as she had expected. It was tender and gentle. Chrissy closed her eyes and relaxed against his arm. Then, into the middle of the kiss, Jeff's laughing face appeared in her thoughts.

Roger drew apart from her, looking at her shyly. *He is so sweet*, Chrissy thought, smiling up at him. *He's like a big, cuddly teddy bear.*

She leaned over and brushed his lips with hers. "I think you're terrific," she whispered. "I should be going now. See you Monday."

As she got out of the car she looked back at him. The way he gazed at her so lovingly and tenderly almost melted her heart. *I couldn't do anything to hurt him*, she thought.

She was already in bed when she heard a car

pull up outside. It stayed there for what seemed like an eternity with the engine still running. Then, finally, Chrissy heard Caroline's light steps on the stairs. She tiptoed into the bedroom and sat down on her bed to remove her shoes.

"Hi, Cara," Chrissy called from her bed.

"Oh, Chrissy, hi. I didn't wake you, did I? I was trying to be so quiet."

"I wasn't asleep. What time is it?"

"After midnight. Have you been home long?"

"About half an hour."

Caroline let out a long sigh. "We went for a drive along the ocean. It was very pretty."

"Sounds romantic," Chrissy said, wishing it had been her driving along the ocean with Jeff.

"It was, very," Caroline admitted. "The waves were all silver, and the breeze was warm. It was just a perfect night. No fog . . . you could even see a big ship way on the horizon."

"You noticed a lot about the scenery," Chrissy commented. "I would have thought that with a guy like Jeff beside you, you wouldn't want to look at anything else."

"So you thought he was cute, huh?"

"Cute? Gorgeous is more like it! Cara—the guy was dynamite."

"I guess he is good-looking," Caroline said hesitantly.

"But he's conceited?"

"Oh, no—he's a really nice person. Fun, too. You saw tonight. He likes to laugh."

"Some people have all the luck," Chrissy remarked. "Finding a guy who looks like that and doesn't think he's Mister Wonderful! Remember Hunter? He was gorgeous, but he knew it! I don't think he ever passed a mirror without touching his hair."

"Oh, Jeff's not like that," Caroline said hastily. "He's funny, but he's nice, too, and he cares a lot about other people. We agree on absolutely everything. He even likes the same sort of music and art . . ."

"Sounds like a match made in heaven," Chrissy admitted grudgingly. "And I take it he's equally good in the kissing department. You were parked outside for a long time."

Caroline was silent for a while. Then she said, "He's a very good kisser, if you want to know," she said. "Just right, in fact—not too shy, but he doesn't come on too strong, either."

"Holy cow, the guy's perfect," Chrissy said. "So are you planning a June wedding?"

Caroline lay back on her bed and gave a big sigh. "There's one problem, Chrissy," she said.

"Which is?"

"I don't feel anything for him," Caroline said bleakly. "Not a single goose bump when he kisses me. He puts his arm around me, and it's like a coat over my shoulders. When Luke only just touched me I felt like I'd got an electric shock." She paused. "Chrissy, do you think I should still keep on dating Jeff?" she asked.

"No!!" Chrissy wanted to yell. "Let me have him!" Instead she heard her own voice saying,

"He sounds so right for you, Caroline. You'd be crazy to give him up."

"I don't understand it myself," Caroline said slowly. "He *is* right for me, in every way. We agree about things, we like doing the same things. If you had to pick a date for me from a computer match-up, it would select Jeff out of all the men in San Francisco! What is wrong with me?"

Chrissy propped herself up on her elbow and looked across at her cousin. The streetlight was shining into their room, making Caroline's hair look silver instead of blond. Chrissy thought she looked like a mermaid sitting on a rock, slim and delicate with her hair tumbling over her shoulders.

"You can't choose who you fall in love with, Cara," she said softly. "If you could, the world would be full of contented couples. There would be no divorces over who watches soap operas and who watches the ball games!"

"I guess you're right," Caroline said at last.

"I know I'm right. Remember Jay, the newspaper editor? He fell desperately in love with me, even though I did nothing to encourage him. Nothing, not once, and yet he couldn't stop thinking about me. You've got the opposite problem right now— you have the go-ahead to fall in love, and you don't want to."

"So what should I do, Chrissy?" Caroline sank back onto her pillows, no longer highlighted in silver.

"You could always hand him over to me," Chrissy said lightly. "I'd take good care of him for you!"

"Thanks a million, that's real sweet of you," Caroline said in an amused voice. "And what about Roger?" she added. "I thought he was really nice, Chrissy. From your description I was expecting a total nerd, but he looked great—and I could tell he was interesting, if a little shy."

"He is," Chrissy said. "He's very nice, and he's interesting, too."

"And you two seem to get along so well," Caroline said hesitantly.

"We do get along well," Chrissy admitted, "except that it's the same for me as it is for you—he doesn't make me tingle all over."

"And he feels more than that for you?"

"I know he does. The way he looked at me when I got out of the car tonight . . ."

"Do you think it would hurt him if you said you wanted to stop dating?"

"Hurt him—it would wipe him out, I know it."

"You were only joking when you said you wanted Jeff, weren't you?"

Chrissy sensed the tension in her cousin's voice, so she acted as if it were only a joke. "Why—are you ready to hand him over?"

Caroline shook her head firmly. "Frankly, I'm not," she said. "If only his smile didn't remind me of Luke so much. Every time he smiles at me, I think it's Luke smiling. I keep hoping that it will turn out just great—that I'll suddenly look at him, and he'll make me tingle the way Luke did." She looked across at Chrissy with a grin. "So, how about you—are you ready to give up Roger?"

Chrissy laughed, determined to keep the whole conversation on a light level and not betray her true thoughts. "I couldn't right now," she said. "I've just got him to dress well and feel good about himself. If I left him at this point, I'd crush his ego. Besides, Roger and I like the same things. We're comfortable together. I could never date a guy like Jeff—I don't know an oboe from my elbow."

Caroline giggled at this. "So it looks like we're stuck the way we are for the moment," she said.

"Looks like it," Chrissy said, "unless you want to give me a quick course on the history of Western music, all the instruments in the orchestra, the names of every symphony orchestra in the world— Stop it!" she yelled as Caroline began pelting her with pillows.

Chapter 13

"Chrissy, are you still with us?" Caroline asked her cousin as they walked home together one afternoon.

"Am I what?" Chrissy jumped as she realized she had only half heard the question.

Caroline laughed. "I wondered if you'd moved to a different planet. I just told you that I got a C minus on my math test, and you said, 'That's nice!' What's on your mind—something you'd like to talk about?"

Chrissy's cheeks flushed bright red. "I-it's nothing, really," she stammered. She could hardly come right out and say, "You see, I can't get your boyfriend out of my mind whatever I do!"

Since she had met Jeff she had tried very hard not to think about him. She still looked forward

to seeing Roger at Dr. Garrison's, but the big
problem was that the warmth she felt with Roger
was nothing compared with the giant charge of
electricity that shot through her whenever she
thought about Jeff. She felt bewitched by Jeff, as
if someone had given her a love potion, and she
couldn't fight it. He had even started creeping
into her dreams at night, and there was nobody
in the world she could tell about it.

*So the only sensible thing is to forget all about
him,* she reminded herself for the millionth time,
wrenching her thoughts back to the present and
back to Caroline.

"At least we'll have partners for the junior
prom," Caroline commented, obviously unaware
of the struggle going on inside Chrissy. "And
money to buy dresses!"

"Oh, yes, the junior prom," Chrissy said. "They
were talking about it in my English class today. I
guess the tickets go on sale next week. I had no
idea proms were such grand things in the city.
Back home they just decorate the gym with
paper streamers, but the kids were talking about
the Sheraton Palace Hotel?"

"Oh, sure," said Caroline. "The junior prom and
senior ball are always in big hotels. Some of the
kids even rent limos to get there, and there is
dinner first at an expensive restaurant, and you
know the guy always wears a tux, and of course
the girl wears a really superglamorous dress. A
prom usually costs a few hundred dollars."

"Wow!" Chrissy said. "What happens if you

don't have that kind of money?"

"You don't come," Caroline admitted. "I agree it's not very fair, but now that we've got jobs we can afford it. Hey, you know what—we could go as a foursome. Won't that be fun?"

The thought of watching Caroline dance cheek to cheek with Jeff didn't sound like fun to Chrissy. In fact, she didn't know how she would stand it, but she managed to smile bravely. "Sure," she agreed. "That'll be great."

"It's a good thing we're working, isn't it?" Caroline asked. "I wonder what Rog will look like in a tux? I bet he'll look really distinguished, like a young doctor. And Jeff will look fantastic," she went on. "How about a light gray tux to show off his tan?"

Chrissy shivered at the thought of it. Caroline sounded excited and animated and didn't seem to notice that Chrissy was not hogging the conversation for once. "I'm so glad I've got Jeff," Caroline admitted. "A lot of the girls were saying they didn't have dates for the prom, and it would be horrible to have to scramble around at the last minute to find a boy you can go with as a friend. Most of the available ones you wouldn't be seen dead with! Tracy is really mad that she broke up with George now. She's wondering if she could put up with him being boring for another evening, just so she has a partner."

"George was pretty boring," Chrissy admitted. "Much too quiet and dull for Tracy."

"Still, he was better than nothing," Caroline

said. "And when it comes to proms, anything is better than nothing."

Chrissy stared down at the cracks in the sidewalk and found her thoughts drifting to the dances back home. The proms there seemed primitive compared with California. Some girls made their dresses, and other borrowed from big sisters and friends. The decorating committee spent hours stapling paper flowers in the gym— all very primitive, the kids here would think. *And yet we have fun at those dances,* Chrissy decided. *I don't even know if I'll feel at ease eating dinner in a very fancy restaurant. I don't think Roger will, either. I wonder if Caroline and Jeff will understand if we don't join them?*

"Do you have to work this afternoon?" Chrissy asked, anxious to move away from the subject of proms.

Caroline nodded. "I don't have to, but I said I would. Mr. Simon is expecting a big shipment of new stuff, and I said I'd help him put it in the stockroom. He doesn't want it cluttering up the store. Are you working today?"

"Only until five," Chrissy said.

"You lucky thing. Think of me and Jeff trudging up and down the stairs to the stockroom. We probably won't get out of there until midnight," Caroline said.

Crazy thoughts started spinning again in Chrissy's mind. "I could come down and give you a hand if you like," she said before she had time to think clearly.

Caroline beamed. "Would you really, Chrissy? That would be so nice of you."

"Sure," Chrissy said. Her imagination was running riot, picturing herself and Jeff alone in a dark stockroom, hands brushing as he took a package from her . . .

"That's great," said Caroline. "And I don't suppose you could bring Roger with you, too?"

"Roger?" The bubble burst.

"I just thought," Caroline said, "I just thought, you know, the more the merrier, and it would make the work go more quickly."

"I don't know if he's busy," Chrissy said hastily. Hands could hardly brush in the stockroom if Roger was one step behind her, could they?

"Ask him at work when you see him," Caroline said.

"He might not show up today," Chrissy said reluctantly. "It's not his official work day, you know."

"So call him as soon as we get home," Caroline insisted. "It'll be fun with the four of us."

Chrissy swallowed hard. "Okay," she said.

Caroline went right to work when they got home from school. Chrissy was tempted not to call Roger at all, then make up a story that he was busy. It would be the easiest thing in the world, after all. Caroline wouldn't ask questions, and everything would work out as she planned it, except . . . except she knew she could never shake the bad taste from her mouth if she lied to

Caroline. With a big sigh she dialed Roger's number.

"Gee, I'd like to help your cousin, but not tonight, Chrissy," Roger's gentle voice replied when she told him the situation. "I have way too much homework—big test in chemistry. In fact, I was kind of hoping you'd help me study"—his voice grew wistful— "but you can't let Caroline down, of course, I understand that. It was nice of you to volunteer to help her."

Chrissy felt very bad. She was glad she had talked to Roger on the phone so that he could not see her face, or she his.

"Look, Rog, if this is important to you—"

"No, no, that's fine, Chrissy. You go. I don't think anyone can really help me study much. I've just got to wade through this whole notebook. I'll survive."

He hung up the phone, leaving Chrissy feeling guilty but relieved. Roger didn't need her to help him study, he had said so. Now she could go to the music store without having him tagging along.

She raced through her chores at the vet's office.

"Heavens, you are Miss Efficiency tonight," Jim Garrison commented. "Are you training for the speed cleaning championship?"

Chrissy laughed. "No, I've got to be somewhere else soon."

"Can't be a date," Jim teased, "because Roger called to say he's studying chemistry."

"No, it's just to help my cousin with some moving," Chrissy said hastily.

"Are you sure you're not turning into a saint?" Jim asked, chuckling as he went out. "I'll be looking out for the halo, you know."

This last remark increased Chrissy's feelings of guilt, which lingered on all the way to the music store. The guilt doubled again when Caroline beamed at her as she came in through the door.

"You are an angel to get here so quickly," she said. "You've no idea how much there is to be done. Look at what arrived in the shipment." She indicated a tower of packages and boxes that reached almost to the ceiling on one side of the store. "We'll be staggering up and down the stairs all night."

"Don't worry, my muscles will make it easy," Chrissy said, grinning as she looked around. "Is Jeff here yet?" she asked casually. "We'll let him carry the really heavy stuff."

Caroline made a face. "He's not coming," she said. "Isn't that a bummer? He called to say his new rock group has got a gig playing at this club in Mill Valley. Apparently they've been hoping to get booked there for the longest time, and the group that should have been playing had to cancel because their lead singer has the flu. He was all excited about the gig, but he did feel bad about not coming in tonight."

"Oh," Chrissy said, swallowing hard and trying not to let her disappointment show.

"So where's Roger?" Caroline asked.

"He couldn't come. He has to study for a chemistry test."

"Oh," Caroline said. Then she smiled. "These boys—where are they when we need them, huh? I guess it's all up to us now, Chrissy."

"Oh, sure," Chrissy mumbled, "all up to us."

It serves me right, Chrissy thought. *I don't know what's happened to me—trying to manipulate my cousin and my boyfriend just for the chance of being with another guy! Maybe I really am bewitched. I am going to get Jeff out of my mind if it's the last thing I do. From now on it's me and Roger, and I'll be perfectly happy about it!*

Chapter 14

Chrissy managed to keep Jeff at the back of her mind for the rest of the week. Whenever he started to creep into her thoughts, her aching muscles were a good reminder of her stupidity.

I'm going to learn to be like Caroline, she decided. *Caroline is so level-headed. You never see her rushing into dumb things without thinking. You never see her getting carried away by a boy she hardly even knows just because he happens to look extra cute.*

She started thinking positively about the junior prom, joining in discussions at school about where to shop for dresses and flowers and the best places to eat. She even had a great idea for the dinner. Instead of going to an expensive restaurant, the boys could come over to the

Kirbys' apartment for a candlelight dinner. She
and Cara could prepare it in advance, and maybe
her aunt and uncle wouldn't mind serving it. She
was sure they'd get a kick out of that. And this
way, they could all save a lot of money, and be
more at ease—except that Jeff would be there.
But she'd just have to learn to handle that.

She ran home from work excitedly. "Caroline?"
she yelled, slamming the front door behind her.
"I've been doing some serious thinking and—"

She broke off in midsentence as she stared at
her cousin. Caroline was walking around the
dining room table with a large book on her head.
Her face was made up like a doll's with bright red
lips and huge black eyelashes, and she was
draped like a Greek goddess with a pink bed-
sheet over one shoulder.

"What are you doing?" Chrissy asked.

"Sshhh!" said Caroline. "You're making me lose
concentration."

"Is there a toga party coming up, or are you
thinking of wearing a sheet to the junior prom?"
Chrissy asked. "That would sure save a bundle."

"Of course I'm not . . ." The book teetered, and
Caroline caught it as it slid off her head. "Now
look what you made me do," she said. "I'd been
around the room five times."

"Is this some sort of San Francisco spring
ritual?" asked Chrissy.

Caroline grinned. "Idiot!" she said. "It's all very
simple, really. I'm practicing to be a model."

"A model? You want to be a model?" Chrissy almost squeaked.

Caroline looked at her coldly. "What's wrong with that? I am tall and slim enough. You have to be five seven, and I'm just about five seven. I think I could be a very good model."

"I'm not saying you couldn't," Chrissy said hastily. "But what gave you the idea? You are one of the last people I'd think of as a model. You hate it when people stare at you."

"I'd get over it. I love nice clothes and being in fashion. Wouldn't it be great to slink down a runway in a thousand-dollar dress?"

"I don't know what's gotten into you," Chrissy said. "We know girls at school who are models. Ask them, ask Dolores—she'll tell you what it's really like. Could you take being treated like a piece of meat?"

"To see my picture in a glossy magazine, I could," Caroline said. "Or in a TV commercial— think about it, Chrissy, wouldn't it be great to do a jeans commercial or swimwear and fly to the Caribbean for a shoot?"

Chrissy pulled out a chair from the dining table and sat down. "You've never mentioned wanting to do anything like this before. Have you been considering it long?"

"About an hour and a half," Caroline said. "It just came to me."

"Came to you how? Were you walking down the street when a voice from heaven said, 'Be a model, Caroline Kirby'?"

Caroline smiled. "Almost," she said. "I was discovered!" She looked shy and proud at the same time. "A talent scout spotted me."

Chrissy looked at her cousin in awe. "No kidding? What did he say?"

"I was just coming out of the music store, and I saw this guy looking at me. I started to hurry off, but he crossed the street and caught up with me. Then, before I could scream or anything, he asked me if I'd ever been a model."

"Go on."

"He said his agency was recruiting new faces, and I had the look that was coming in."

"Cara, that's fantastic!" Chrissy tried to feel genuinely happy for her cousin, although she couldn't help a twinge of jealousy. Why hadn't a talent scout ever stopped her? "So what happened then? Did he sign you up on the spot?"

"I've got to go down to the agency after school tomorrow and meet the big shots," Caroline said. "Isn't it exciting, Chrissy? I've dreamed of things like this happening, but I never thought it really would. It's almost too good to be true."

Chrissy studied her cousin's face. It was glowing with excitement. "So you think you'll be giving up the music store?" she asked.

"Oh, sure," Caroline said. "As soon as I start work as a model. I won't need it anymore. Trevor told me—"

"Trevor?"

"He's the scout. He's very cute, Chrissy. Really sophisticated. I think I understand what you were saying about older men. He knows just the right thing to say to make a girl feel special." Caroline's eyes opened wide as she continued in a voice filled with wonder. "And you know what's really fantastic? He looks so much like Luke. I almost fell through the floor when he smiled at me. And do you know the agency handles the account for a cruise line, and they send models on their cruises?"

"Sounds fabulous, Cara," Chrissy said. "Soon you'll be mingling with the show biz crowd. So what happens to Jeff?"

Chrissy had a fleeting vision of herself dancing in Jeff's arms at the prom. No, she realized, that would never happen. She had already promised to go to the prom with Roger.

"Oh, Jeff," Caroline said as if she had only just remembered his name. "You know, Jeff and I have never really clicked. I mean, I like him. I really like him, and of course I've already talked to him about the junior prom, although I bet Trevor would look great in a tux!"

"Caroline Kirby! Remember what fun you made of me because I fell for Dr. Garrison? Now you're doing the same thing," Chrissy scolded. "And for Pete's sake, you only met this guy for five minutes. You know nothing about him."

"I know that he's . . . well, he's different, Chrissy. The way he looked at me made me feel really special—as if I'm the girl he's been looking for all his life. You know how empty I've felt since I left Luke. I really tried hard with Jeff, but I've been wondering if maybe I hadn't got it all wrong. Maybe Jeff wasn't the right one, but Trevor is?"

"Oh, come on, Cara," Chrissy said uneasily. "You can't just make a decision about a guy by looking at him and deciding he's cute."

"I know," Caroline said, "but I can't help being excited about this. Nothing like it has ever happened to me before. Imagine me, a high-fashion model, on the cover of magazines, up on billboards . . . Maybe I am jumping ahead too far. Maybe the owners of the agency will meet me and decide I'm not right after all. That's why I was practicing my walk. Do you think I'm slinky enough?"

"Cara, they won't want you to be slinky. They'll want an ordinary teenager. Just be yourself."

"What should I wear? *Mama mìa*, I'm so nervous. I must make the right impression."

"Let's go into the bedroom, and I'll help you choose," Chrissy said. "Although if I were you, I'd wear something really simple, like your white jeans and the striped sailor top. You look nice and young and friendly in those."

"But do they want young and friendly? What if they are looking for mature and slinky?"

"Caroline, the guy would never have come up to you in the first place if they'd wanted mature and slinky!" Chrissy said, laughing. She got up and walked across the room. "If he'd have picked *me*, I could have understood it," she added, pushing her hair across her face and wiggling her hips until she made Caroline burst out laughing.

Chrissy couldn't wait for Caroline to get back from the interview after school the next day. For the first time she was glad she wasn't working so she could be the first to hear Cara's news. She paced up and down the front steps of the apartment house until Tracy threatened to tie her feet together.

"But I can't relax until she gets back," Chrissy pleaded. "I do hope she got it. Imagine us knowing a famous model."

"Maybe you'll have to pay to speak to her," Tracy joked. "I can't believe it! Who would ever have thought of Caroline as a model? She never seemed the type to me."

"She's pretty," Chrissy said.

"Oh, sure, but you're pretty. Lots of people are pretty. Models are different, though. Look at Dolores—she's a typical model. She walks as if she wants people to watch her. She always has. Cara blushes if people stare at her. Why would anyone pick her out of a crowd, I wonder?"

"She has the look that's coming in, apparently," Chrissy said. "I'm so excited for her."

"Me too," Tracy said. "If she has the look they want now, that's great. Now will you stand still for a moment, I'm getting dizzy watching you."

"I'm getting restless. I think maybe I'll pop down to the bank," Chrissy said. "I have my paycheck to deposit." She paused and grinned at Tracy. "Doesn't that sound wonderful? I love going to pay in money instead of taking it out all the time. It's great to be a working woman."

"Just think of what Caroline will be making soon," Tracy mused.

"I am thinking," Chrissy said. "Compared to ninety dollars an hour, four fifty doesn't sound so hot, but it's a lot better than nothing. I can even go to the aquarium with the biology class next week!"

Tracy gave her a little push. "If you're going to the bank, you'd better go or it'll be next week already."

"You want to come with me?"

"No, I'll stay here and wait for Cara," Tracy replied. "I hope she gets back soon, the suspense is killing me now."

Chrissy walked briskly down the hill, scanning the sidewalks with her eyes, hoping to see Caroline on her way home. *Maybe she'll take a taxi now that she's going to be rich and famous,* Chrissy thought. *Imagine, taking taxis and popping into elegant restaurants whenever you want to.*

She reached the bank and deposited her check. The teller even smiled at her and called her Miss Madden, which made her feel very important. She was just on her way out again when she did a double take. Caroline was standing at the counter, so busy filling in forms that she didn't notice Chrissy. Chrissy hurried over to her and stood, patiently waiting, until Caroline had finished her transaction.

She heard the teller say, "And you want to withdraw all of it?"

Caroline's voice sounded breathless when she answered, "That's right. All of it."

"How would you like it—in hundred-dollar bills or smaller?"

"It doesn't matter. Hundreds will do."

Chrissy watched the clerk count out hundred-dollar bills, then she watched Caroline take them carefully, fold them, and put them into her wallet. As she turned to leave Chrissy stepped in front of her. Caroline's face turned a rich crimson.

"Chrissy—what are you doing here?" she asked.

"Depositing in my paycheck. How did it go?"

Caroline beamed. "Chrissy—they want me. They say I can be a great model someday. All I need is a little training."

"What kind of training?" Chrissy asked.

"You know—I need to learn how to walk on a catwalk, how to apply makeup, how to choose accessories—all that kind of stuff."

"And where are you going to get this training?" Chrissy fell into step beside Caroline as they came out of the bank.

"That's what's so wonderful," Caroline said. "They have a modeling school right on the premises. I can go to classes there, and when I'm ready, they'll move me across to the agency. Doesn't that sound great?"

"Oh, sure," Chrissy said. "And they'll train you for free?"

"Of course not," Caroline said, looking defensive for the first time. "I have to pay for the training, but they say I can make all the money back in my first four jobs."

"So the training's expensive, then?"

Caroline shrugged her shoulders uneasily. "Pretty expensive," she said. "Five hundred dollars, actually. Then I need photos, too. The whole thing will run about a thousand, but I'll be making ninety dollars an hour. I'll soon pay it back."

Chrissy cleared her throat. "Cara, I don't mean to pry," she said, "but did you just take out all your savings right then?"

"What if I did?" Caroline asked sharply. "It's my money."

"But I thought you said that was an account you had started for college."

Caroline looked at her cousin. "If I'm a successful model, I might not even want to go to college," she said. She swept down the steps of the bank, tossing back her long blond hair as the wind caught it.

"But Cara"—Chrissy ran to keep up with her—"don't you think you should talk to your folks about something as important as this?"

Caroline turned to frown at Chrissy. "I know what they'll say. They'll say that college comes first and modeling is for the birds, but they're wrong. I told you I'd been looking for something I wanted to do with my life—well, finally a door has opened for me, and I'm not going to let anybody stand in my way!"

"N-no, Cara," Chrissy stammered. She wasn't

used to this new, aggressive side to her cousin. "It's just that—"

Caroline grabbed her arm firmly. "Look, Chrissy," she said, "promise me you won't say a thing about any of this to my folks! I don't want them to know until I'm a trained, working model and have replaced my savings. Promise me!"

"No, I won't promise," Chrissy objected. "Cara, be sensible. This is your whole future at stake here."

"That's right, it's *my* future," Caroline stressed. "And I think you're jealous of me, Chrissy Madden, because I got spotted and you didn't. Now promise me you won't tell."

"Okay, I promise," Chrissy said uneasily. "I just hope you know what you're doing."

"For once in my life I'm doing something!" Caroline said. "I'm not relying on my mom or dad or anybody else to get me started. This is going to be all me—I'm going to be responsible for my own success, Chrissy." She glanced down at her watch. "Oh, no, is that the time? I've got to rush. I promised Trevor I'd be back with the money today. I'll see you, Chrissy."

Chrissy opened her mouth to say something, but Caroline touched her arm. "Don't worry, Chrissy. I know what I'm doing—this might seem like life in the fast lane for someone from Danbury, Iowa, but this is the big city. Trust me, everything's going to be just great!" Then she ran off, leaving Chrissy staring after her, swallowing the lump that kept coming into her throat.

Chapter 15

The next afternoon Chrissy stood with Tracy in the alleyway, staring up at a grimy brick building.

"Is this supposed to be the model agency?" Tracy asked, shivering in the deep shadow of the alley.

Chrissy nodded. "See what I mean—would you put a model agency in a place like this?"

"I'm glad we came together," Tracy said. "I'd never have the nerve to go up those stairs alone."

"I hope this works," Chrissy said. "I hope I didn't walk down Market Street looking like this for nothing. There were two cute boys on that last corner, and they laughed at me. Cara had better appreciate this!"

Tracy giggled nervously. "Well, you're not exactly looking your regular self," she said, eyeing

Chrissy critically. Chrissy glanced at her image in a blackened glass window. She did look truly horrible, she had to admit. Tracy's purple sweater was stuffed with a couple of pillows to make her look very heavy. Tracy's tight black miniskirt did not go with the sweater at all, and neither did the heavy red beads. She had braided her hair tightly around her head like an old German doll and wore no makeup, except for some purple under her eyes and some red daubs to give her pimples.

"I had no idea I could ever look so disgusting," Chrissy agreed. "I really do look twenty pounds overweight."

"And I look impossibly short," Tracy said. Chrissy glanced over Tracy's outfit—the flat shoes, the broad horizontal stripes in orange and black that made her look like a bumblebee, the ratty hair, and her father's heavy glasses.

"Okay, let's do it," Chrissy said bravely. "The look of the future is about to be discovered!" With that she clomped clumsily up the stairs.

At the top of the stairs they opened a frosted-glass door and found themselves standing in a very glamorous reception room. It had a plush white carpet and big pots of plants between chrome furniture. The walls were covered in large photos of glamorous models. Chrissy began to wonder if they had made a terrible mistake and this was a genuine model agency. How stupid she would feel when they told her to get lost and not waste their time.

Just then a receptionist appeared. "You're interested in our modeling course?" she asked, looking at them as if they were two slimy things she had just found under a stone. "May I ask who referred you to us?"

"Oh, a girl at our school mentioned she had just signed up here, and she told us about all the money she'd be making," Chrissy babbled, the words coming out in a torrent as they always did when she was nervous. The receptionist's mouth twitched in a smile. "Please take a seat," she said. "I'll see if Mr. Trevor is available to interview you."

The girls sat together on a chrome-and-leather sofa. "So what do you think?" Tracy whispered. "Is this legit or not?"

"I can't tell. It may be," Chrissy whispered back. She gazed at the glamorous photos on the walls. "Hey, that's Christy Brinkley," she whispered to Tracy. "They can't have her on their books! Maybe they are phonies, just like we thought!"

Then the inner door opened, and Trevor came out. Chrissy could see right away what Caroline had found attractive about him. He looked like a citified version of Luke. He had the same dark, hollow-cheeked look, but his hair was perfectly styled, and he was wearing an elegant linen blazer with pale blue striped pants. His shirt was open-necked to reveal a dark tan. When he smiled at them he revealed a mouthful of perfect teeth.

"Hello, girls," he said in an English accent. "So you want to be models, do you? Well, you've come to the right place. I'm Trevor, and you are . . . ?"

"This is Henrietta, and I'm Irmintrude," Chrissy said. She heard Tracy snort at her choice of names.

Trevor's smile did not waver. "Pretty names for two pretty girls," he said. "We've had so many lovely girls sign up with us in the past few weeks. I don't know where all this talent is suddenly coming from."

"Er, Mr. Trevor," Tracy stammered, "we want you to be honest with us. We know that we're not perfect right now. Do you really think we can make it as models someday?"

"Why, sure, darling," Trevor said, perching himself on the arm of the sofa beside her. "You both have a certain something. In fact, you have the look that's coming in right now. There's nothing wrong with you that a little training won't put right."

"Training?" Chrissy asked. "You mean we couldn't join your agency right away?"

Trevor's startling dark eyes turned on her. "All our models have to have our special look," he said. "So we put everyone through our own special grooming course. You'd need to know a little more about makeup and hairstyling, and of course we'd prescribe our own, personalized diet for you, if you needed it."

"And how long would this take?" Chrissy asked. "I'm just dying to be out there modeling."

"No more than a few weeks," Trevor said. "We

can even give you our accelerated course, if you're willing to come in every evening. You'll be on that catwalk by July at the latest, I guarantee it."

"In writing?" Tracy asked.

"What?"

"I asked if you guarantee in writing that we'll get modeling jobs with your agency when we've finished the course," Tracy repeated.

The smiled flickered for a moment on Trevor's lips. "Oh, come on, honey. You wouldn't find an agency in the city who would give you a guarantee like that. So much depends on the state of the market. If the customers are buying, I can keep every girl on the books working. If it's a dry spell, you might have to wait a few weeks before you get your first job." He paused and ran his tongue over his lips. "But you'll be working. Don't you worry about it. Before you know it, you'll be on a cruise ship or modeling swimwear in the Caribbean. Just think of it, girls . . . soft scented nights, waves lapping, all that money in your pockets to spend . . . Lots of our girls buy themselves a new sports car when they get back from a Caribbean assignment. I'm always spotting them driving around town in their Porsches and Ferraris." He paused and looked at the girls with anticipation. "So, are you ready to sign up? We've only got a few forms that need your signatures. If you sign today, I think we can still get you in on our next training session, but I've only got two slots open.

If you leave it till tomorrow, you might have to wait until June to start."

"Er, Mr. Trevor—could we see the school and meet the teachers before we sign?" Chrissy asked innocently. "I'd really like to discuss the subjects we'll study before I decide."

"Why, of course you can, darling," Trevor said, giving her a beaming smile. "There's nobody at the school right now, of course, because most of our classes are in the evenings. But I tell you what—you come by tomorrow evening, and I'll have a teacher available to answer all your questions. You can put down your deposit then, too. Only a hundred dollars will secure you a place in the class. And you don't have to pay the rest right away, although we do give a good discount for cash."

There was a pause as Trevor looked from one to the other. "So how about it, girls? Are we ready to make history? Are we ready to take our chance of a lifetime?"

"We'd like to think it over," Tracy said hesitantly. "Talk it over with our folks, I mean."

"You don't have much time for dilly-dallying," Trevor said. "Remember what I said about only two places left on our next course. And I should mention that the students from that course will have graduated just in time for our biggest jeans commercial. Lots of famous models got discovered in that last year."

The phone rang, and Trevor paused as the receptionist answered it. "I'm glad you called back," she said into the phone. "I think we still have places free." She looked over at Trevor. "Are those two places still free on the course?" she asked. "Or are these girls taking them. I have someone here who wants to sign up."

"So how about it, girls?" Trevor asked. "Don't lose your chance."

"It's okay. You can give the place to the girl on the phone," Chrissy said. "My dad is a lawyer, and I'm sure he'd want to look into any contract. . . ."

The smile vanished from Trevor's face as if somebody had wiped it off. "A lawyer, eh?" he asked, his accent sounding suddenly more New York than London. "Well, you'd better talk it over with him, then. Maybe he wouldn't want his daughter being a model. It's a dog-eat-dog world, you know. No good for a sensitive girl like yourself. No, somehow I don't think you'd be right for a model after all. Of course, you could use our charm school course, but I wouldn't want to push you into anything."

"And what about me?" Tracy asked. "Do I still get to be a model? I'm not at all sensitive."

"Why don't you do the training and find out, sweetheart," he said pleasantly to Tracy. "Of course, we don't have that much call for the ethnic look, if you know what I mean, but if we ever have any Chinese commercials, you can bet that you'd be hired!"

The two girls walked down the steps and back into the open air. When they were safely around the corner, lost in the anonymity of Market

Street, they looked at each other for the first time and burst into giggles.

"Boy, what a total phony," Tracy said.

"Did you see his face when I said my dad was a lawyer?" Chrissy asked.

"That was pure genius," Tracy said admiringly. "After he heard that he couldn't wait to get you out of there."

"And what about you and your ethnic commercials?" Chrissy said, laughing even harder.

"At least now Caroline will have to believe us that Trevor's a phony," Tracy said. "We've even got those Polaroid pictures of ourselves to show her. I just hope she can make them give her her money back."

"They'll have to," Chrissy said. "She's under eighteen, isn't she? She can't even sign a valid contract without her parents' signatures."

"Besides, we'll threaten them with your dad the lawyer," Tracy said, chuckling. "I don't think we'll have any trouble at all."

"Thanks for your help, Tracy," Chrissy said. "I'd never have dared do any of this alone."

Tracy grinned. "It was fun, wasn't it? My biggest problem was not bursting out laughing all the time. Especially when you said your name was Irmintrude! I could have died."

"It was the first weird name that came to mind," Chrissy said. "My uncle had a cow called Irmintrude once. Come on, let's hurry back to your house. People keep staring at us."

Later that evening Chrissy finally confronted

Caroline. She waited until they were in their room alone together, then handed Caroline the photograph. "Here," she said. "Look at this."

Caroline looked, stared harder, then burst out laughing. "Chrissy, is this you and Tracy?" she asked. "You look terrible! What are you dressed up for, Halloween practice?"

"No," Chrissy said quietly, "we're dressed for an interview with a modeling agency."

"A what?" Caroline looked up from the photo, still laughing.

"We went to sign on as models," Chrissy said. "We figured if you could make all this money, we'd like to do it, too."

Caroline's face looked half-amused, half-puzzled. "But why dress up like that? No agency in its right mind would ever consider you looking like freaks."

"One did," Chrissy said evenly. "We were told that we had the look that was coming in."

"Who on earth would tell you a think like that?" Caroline asked, still amused and puzzled. "Look at you, Chrissy—you look totally disgusting in this photo, and Tracy looks real dumpy."

"A Mr. Trevor told us," Chrissy said quietly. "He said if we had a few lessons, we could be top models. In fact, he did his best to persuade us to sign up today. Only he lost interest when I told him that my father was a lawyer."

The smile faded from Caroline's face, and she went very white. "Trevor said all that? My Trevor?"

Chrissy nodded. "Your Trevor."

Caroline stared at her with large, scared eyes. "So he really was a phony?" she asked.

"It sure looks that way," Chrissy said. "I'm sorry if I butted into your life, Cara, but it all sounded too good to be true. I had to find out if you were throwing your money away for nothing."

"And it looks like I was," Caroline said. "Oh, Chrissy, what am I going to do? Do you think he'll give me my money back if I say that I've changed my mind?"

"I think he will if I come with you, dressed normally, with this photo as evidence. After all, you are under age. I'll just mention my father the lawyer again, and I bet he can't give you your money quickly enough."

Caroline sank onto the bed and buried her head in her hands. "I made a big fool of myself, didn't I?" she asked in a cracked voice.

"How could you know?" Chrissy said kindly. "It sounded like a genuine offer that was too good to turn down."

"I really believed everything he said," Caroline said hopelessly. "He sounded so convincing. He really seemed to think that I was special."

"He was a very persuasive sort of person," Chrissy said. "Anyone would have been flattered if a guy like Trevor had picked them from the whole of San Francisco."

"I should have known better," Caroline muttered. "I don't know what came over me—I just took one look at him, and he seemed so . . ."

"So like Luke?" Chrissy asked gently.

Caroline nodded.

Chrissy touched her arm. "Cara, you're going to have to make a big effort to let go of Luke," she said. "You'll never find another guy just like him. All the things that made him special were because of what's inside him, not only because of the way he looked. Maybe you need to go out with boys who are totally different from him for a while."

Caroline nodded sadly. "You're right," she said earnestly. "I have got to get him out of my system. If I could only think of a nice, different boy who was not already taken. . . ." She paused, then shook her head. "What a dummy I've been. Like you said, it was too good to be true. I'm not the model type, am I? I've always known that. A little voice in my head kept whispering that all the time I was signing up. That's why I did everything in such a hurry, I think, because I didn't want to listen to the voice in my head."

"That was your common sense," Chrissy said. "Usually it's a very big voice in your head. I don't know how you managed to stifle it this time. Rushing off and withdrawing all your money is the crazy sort of thing I'd do, but not you. It wasn't like you at all."

"I know," said Caroline. She looked up into Chrissy's face. "It's funny, ever since you came here I've always admired the way you rush into things without worrying. I think subconsciously I was trying to be like you. I wanted to take a chance and do something entirely on my own for once. And look where it got me. I'll be a laughingstock around school."

Chrissy put a gentle hand on her cousin's shoulder. "Only Tracy and I know, and we won't blab," she said. "We're just glad we got you out in time."

"So am I. Oh, Chrissy, imagine having to explain all that money to my parents! You guys are really terrific, to do that for me. I owe you one, Chrissy."

Chrissy grinned. "Can I have that in writing, please?"

"No way!" Caroline exclaimed. "I'm not signing anything until I consult my lawyer."

Chapter 16

Chrissy let herself in quietly through the back door of Dr. Garrison's office the next afternoon. Standing in the supply room putting on her white lab coat, she felt a surge of peace and contentment. It felt good to be in a place where she knew where everything was, she knew the routine, she liked the people she worked with, and she even enjoyed the work. No, even if she was spotted by a *real* talent scout, she wouldn't trade this for modeling, she decided. She still didn't know if she wanted a lifetime career as a vet, but being a vet's assistant certainly suited her for now. She broke off from her thoughts and looked up as Roger came into the room.

"Oh, Chrissy, there you are," he said, beaming at her. "I'm so glad you're here."

"Well, thanks, Rog," she replied. "Nice to know I'm needed."

Roger looked at her seriously. "You don't ever have to doubt that while I'm around," he said.

Chrissy smiled self-consciously and busied herself with tidying up the supply room.

"Actually, there is something rather special that I need you for this weekend," he went on.

"What's that?"

"Well," Roger began hesitantly, "I've volunteered to help out at the Marine Mammal Center this Saturday. You see, there's a serious sea lion epidemic. Apparently they're finding sick sea lions on all the local beaches, and the center just can't handle them all." He paused and took a deep breath. "We need all the help we can get, so I was wondering if you'd want to come, too."

"Sure," Chrissy said. "I've never seen a sea lion close up. That'll be interesting."

"Thanks, Chrissy. I knew I could count on you," Roger said, giving her an awkward pat on the back. "This epidemic is spreading like wildfire. If they don't catch and isolate the sick sea lions, the whole colony could be wiped out."

"Wow," Chrissy said. "Those poor sea lions. I hope we can save them."

"Me too," Roger said, shaking his head sadly. He looked over at Chrissy, then down at his sneakers. "Uh, Chrissy, we need all the help we can get at the Marine Mammal Center, so maybe you could ask your cousin to come on Saturday, too."

"I'll see if she's free," Chrissy replied. "She

needs something to take her mind off things right now—although I don't know how she feels about sea lions. She's not really an animal kind of person," she added, remembering all too clearly Caroline's misadventures on the farm during spring break. An enormous pig had chased her, a friendly cow had charged at her, and a flock of angry chickens had attacked her. After all that, Chrissy wasn't sure how Caroline would react to helping a band of sick sea lions.

She caught sight of her cousin climbing into Jeff's car as she came home from work that evening.

"Cara, wait up!" she yelled, sprinting up the hill toward her.

Caroline waited patiently, one foot already in the car. "What's wrong, Chrissy?" she asked.

"Nothing's wrong," Chrissy panted as she reached the car. "I just needed to talk to you. Hi, Jeff." She tried hard not to look at him as she spoke because she knew she wouldn't be able to look away.

"Hi, Chrissy," Jeff said in his smooth, deep voice that melted her all the way down to her toes. She had to glance at him then and found that she hadn't gotten over him one little bit. No doubt about it, he was pure, one hundred percent gorgeous. *How Caroline cannot melt into jelly every time she looks at him, I'll never understand,* she thought. *She still acts as if she's dating some goober who's only just better than nothing.*

"So what was so important, Chrissy?" Caroline asked.

"Er—what?" Chrissy forced herself out of the trance that Jeff's smile had thrown her into. "Oh—what I wanted to talk to you about." She gave Caroline a big smile. "I wanted to see if you were possibly free on Saturday?"

"Got something exciting in mind?" Jeff asked.

She hadn't considered the possibility of having Jeff along before. She didn't think that would be such a wise idea, but there was no way out now.

"Pretty exciting," she heard herself saying. "You see, there's an epidemic among the sea lions, and they need help at the Marine Mammal Center to round them up. Roger and I are going along, and he says they need as many helpers as possible."

Caroline looked at Chrissy as if she couldn't believe her ears. "You want us to round up sea lions?" she asked. "Chrissy, you know what those chickens did to me. I don't think I could cope with two hundred pounds of blubber chasing me down the beach!"

Chrissy heard Jeff chuckle from inside the car. "That would be worth seeing," he said. "Why don't we go, Cara? We didn't have anything special planned for the weekend."

"I thought we were going to take a picnic out to the Headlands on Saturday," Caroline said.

"We still could. We'll help round up the sea lions, and then we'll go on the picnic," he suggested.

"I don't know, Jeff," Caroline said hesitantly.

"I'm not very good around animals."

"But just think of the poor sea lions, Cara," Chrissy pleaded. "They might all be wiped out if we don't stop this disease now. You care about saving things, don't you? You fought hard enough to save those old houses and the park near the school. How about poor cuddly sea lions?"

"I don't know, Chrissy," Caroline said hesitantly. "I do care. I don't want the sea lions to be wiped out, but . . ." She turned to Jeff. "Do you really think we should go?"

"Sure, why not," Jeff said. "It'll be a new experience. I can just see myself lassoing sea lions! Why don't we all ride out together in my car on Saturday morning?"

"Great," said Chrissy, her heart pounding at the prospect of spending a whole day with Jeff. *Stop it, Chrissy*, she told herself sternly. Out loud she added, "I'll tell Roger. We'd better get an early start."

"Okay, cowboy," Jeff agreed, mimicking John Wayne. "Let's go round up them sea lions."

Chrissy could see his laughing face as the car drove away. *That guy knows how to have a good time*, she thought. *I bet he's a fun person to be with*. She gazed after him wistfully, remembering that on Saturday she would be with Roger, and that Roger would be crushed if she paid any attention to Jeff.

On Saturday morning, Chrissy and Roger and Caroline and Jeff joined the rest of the volunteers on the windy seashore. Although the city had been bathed in sunlight, a chill fog still swirled around the beaches, making everyone turn up their collars and clap their hands together to keep warm. Chrissy had even brought her ski cap with her just in case her ears froze up.

She looked around at the variety of people gathered on the beach. She noticed lots of kids her own age, but also many older men and women and families with children. She even saw a pair of guys with long hair and leather jackets park their motorcycles and come over to help out.

A young man in a black parka was yelling out instructions. "I need about ten of you to move our young sea lions from the nursery to a new site out of contact with the infected ones," he called. He pointed to Chrissy's foursome and another group. "You guys will do. Go with Roger. He'll show you what we need done."

Chrissy noticed Roger stand up tall when his name was mentioned. He began to march in the direction of some old army huts. "This way," he called, waving a hand as if he were a tour guide.

Chrissy ran to catch up with him. "I didn't realize you were an expert," she remarked.

"I told you I worked out here all last summer," Roger said, looking a little embarrassed. "I still come out whenever I get a chance."

They stopped in front of a small holding tank. "These are teenage sea lions," Roger said, addressing the people who had followed him. "They were last winter's babies who were brought in abandoned. We are planning to release them this fall, so it's important they don't get sick now." Six pairs of large brown eyes peered up hopefully from the water. The most adventurous sea lion climbed up on the rim of the tank.

"Aren't they sweet?" Chrissy whispered to Caroline. "Even you couldn't be frightened of them."

Caroline smiled. "They are darling," she whispered back. "Just look at those fuzzy whiskers. They look like little old men."

"Where are we taking them?" asked a slender woman. "They look pretty heavy."

"We have a new temporary tank for them down at the other end of the beach," Roger said. "We're going to wrap the more restless kids in sacking, and we'll hold the rest of the babies, then we'll move all of them down in the truck."

Chrissy looked at Roger in surprise. He no longer looked awkward or klutzy. He seemed so secure and confident now, and his enthusiasm was catching.

"Can I start off with a baby?" Caroline asked, moving close to Roger.

Roger took her arm. "Come on, I'll show you what to do. It's no problem once you know how." The group followed him into the tank area, where he lifted a struggling baby sea lion and handed it to Chrissy and Jeff, who happened to be standing on his other side. "This is Pongo, he's good-natured, so he can go straight into the truck." Chrissy and Jeff struggled with the heavy body and put him on the truck bed.

"Hey, Cara," Jeff called as Caroline approached, carrying the smallest sea lion, bundled up in sacking with just its little brown nose and whiskers showing. "How about this?" He put his sunglasses on the sea lion's nose. "He's a celebrity in disguise."

Chrissy giggled at the sea lion's funny expression as he sat there without moving a muscle, but Caroline looked horrified. "Jeff, don't do that—you might scare him."

"Oh, sure, he looks terrified," Jeff said, glancing at Chrissy.

"I know what he needs," Chrissy said, pulling her woolen ski cap out of her jacket pocket and placing it on the sea lion's head. "Now he's a ski lion!" She and Jeff burst out laughing, and the sea lion beamed at them, enjoying the attention.

"Will you two behave yourselves and start taking this seriously!" Caroline said, sounding like a schoolteacher. "We are here to save animals, not have a good time."

"We could try doing both," Jeff suggested.

Chrissy noted as they loaded up the last of the babies onto the truck that Roger continued to give Caroline instructions on the care of sea lions. "If you enjoy working with the young ones, then perhaps you'd want to come with me to the sick nursery," he said.

"Oh, I'd like that," Caroline replied eagerly as she went off with Roger.

"She'll have enough information by the end of the day to last her a lifetime," Chrissy commented casually to Jeff. Inside, though, she didn't feel so calm. *Alone with Jeff at last!* she thought. Then she thought again, *Chrissy Madden, you behave yourself.* Aloud she added, "When Roger gets going on a favorite topic, it's hard to shut him up—and marine mammals are his very favorite topic."

"She seemed interested," Jeff said, following her with his eyes.

Chrissy smiled. "Knowing Cara, she was just being polite. She could tell how much Roger was dying to show off his knowledge to someone."

"Did you want to join them in the sick nursery?" Jeff asked.

Chrissy shrugged and avoided Jeff's gaze. "I don't mind," she said. "How about you?"

"I kind of wanted to do something more adventurous," Jeff confessed. "You know, rounding up wild sea lions—cowboy of the seashore!" He swung an imaginary lasso.

"Okay," said Chrissy. "Let's go join the posse if you want to."

They walked in silence back to the Marine Mammal headquarters.

"I need real strong people to round up these sea lions for their immunization shots," the group leader said, giving Chrissy a scowl.

"Mister, I've given shots to an entire farm full of hogs," Chrissy said, scowling back at him, "and there's nothing more ornery than a hog."

The man looked at her in surprise, then

laughed. "You're hired," he said. "Jump on the truck."

Soon Chrissy and Jeff and several other volunteers were bumping over fire trails, and hugging the cliff tops of the seashore as they looked for wild sea lions. Whenever they spotted any, the leader would halt the truck, and everyone would leap out and trap the sea lions under special nets. If the sea lion was sick, with inflamed, watering eyes and rasping breath, it was secured and put into the truck. If it was well, it was given a shot and released.

"This is more like it," Jeff yelled, flinging a net on top of a large bull sea lion who was trying to head for the ocean. "Hey, Chrissy, come and help me with this one."

After a long morning, they drove back to the headquarters to deliver three sick sea lions to the veterinarians. There was not one volunteer who was not wet, dirty, bruised, and tired, but they were still laughing and hurling insults at each other with the familiarity of team members.

"You want to stay on her good side!" the group leader commented to Jeff. "I bet she packs a mean punch." He laughed as he walked off, and Chrissy blushed as she noticed Jeff's wide grin.

She looked around, pretending to be occupied. "I don't see any sign of Caroline and Roger," she commented. "I expect he's still lecturing on the respiratory system of the sea lion."

Jeff continued to look at her. "I don't know

about you, but I'm starving," he said. "That was hard work back there."

"It certainly was," Chrissy agreed. "I think I've strained every muscle in my arms and shoulders. Those critters are strong!"

"You're not so weak yourself," Jeff said, his blue eyes looking at her intensely. "I was very impressed. I'd never have been able to shoot that needle into the huge bull sea lion the way you did."

Chrissy shrugged. "It wasn't hard," she said. "You don't really need much strength for it."

"But you need guts," Jeff said. "Look, they're serving coffee over there. Let's get some and then find our picnic."

"Shouldn't we wait for Cara and Roger?" Chrissy asked as Jeff carried the picnic cooler from the car.

He grinned. "We probably should, but I'm starved. Come on." And he took her hand as if it were the most natural thing in the world.

Chrissy was not even conscious of her feet touching the ground as she walked up the grassy slope beside him. The last remnants of the fog had melted away, and the hillsides were bathed in clear light. Clumps of brilliant yellow-and-purple lupines were in full bloom, and their sweet fragrance mingled with the tangy scent of the ocean. Chrissy sank down contentedly on the grass.

"This is just perfect," she said, gazing out at the deep blue water. "Look how far you can see today."

Jeff followed Chrissy's gaze, then looked back at her. "Gorgeous," he said. He poked a hand into the cooler and pulled out a large deli sandwich. "Here," he said. "You take the biggest. You worked harder than me." His hand brushed against hers as she took the sandwich from him.

Get a grip on yourself, Chrissy Madden, she told herself firmly. *You are sitting here with Caroline's boyfriend. Remember that.*

"I wonder what happened to Cara and Roger?" she said, fumbling with the wrapper on the sandwich.

Jeff leaned down on one elbow, very close to her. "Are you missing him right now?" he asked in a low but teasing voice.

"Me—missing him?" she repeated in surprise. "He's ... I mean, he's just a good friend." She glanced up at him quickly.

"Are you missing Caroline?" she asked.

Jeff took a deep breath. "I get the feeling that Caroline and I have never clicked somehow. She's really nice, but there's no electricity there—you know what I mean?"

"I know exactly what you mean," Chrissy said.

"And electricity is very important, if you want a real relationship, don't you agree?" he asked.

His face was very close to hers now, and she couldn't help but be mesmerized by his steady blue gaze. "Very important," she said, not even blinking.

"For example," Jeff continued, "I get the feeling there is a whole power station of electricity flowing around here right now. Am I right?"

Chrissy could only nod as he brought his lips gently toward hers. When he kissed her it was exactly how she had imagined it would be. She was floating, out of time and space. She relaxed in his arms, and when she opened her eyes again he was smiling.

"I'm glad I came here today," he said, "or we'd never have known."

Chrissy continued to gaze at him as if she couldn't really believe this were true. *If this is a dream, I don't want to wake up!* she thought.

"Do you know what I'd like to do?" he asked. "I'd like to take a long walk with you along the beach. Do you think they could manage the sea lions without us?"

Chrissy wavered—torn between wanting to be with Jeff at any price and letting down Cara and Roger. Duty finally won. "I guess I promised I'd help out today," she said. "Besides, I wouldn't want to make Cara and Roger feel uncomfortable."

Jeff nodded, reaching out with a finger to stroke her nose. "You are not only cute and strong, but dedicated, too," he said. "Just what I like in a girl."

Chrissy flushed. She was thinking of Caroline. "Oh, well, um, I also have a terrible temper," she stammered. *Maybe if I tell him all my faults, he'll decide that he likes Cara better after all,* she thought. She hated the idea, but for Cara's sake . . . "I also rush into things, and I'm untidy and pigheaded, and I probably talk more than anyone else you've ever met."

Jeff laughed. "Sounds like fun," he said. "I look forward to finding out more. Do you think we could go for that beach walk tomorrow?"

Chrissy looked down to the seashore below, where figures, small as ants, were milling around in the parking lot. She still could not see Cara's bright red sweatshirt or Roger's tall figure among them. "I'd like to," she said, "but it's just that—I can't go behind Cara's back . . . or Roger's."

"I'll talk to Cara tonight," Jeff said. "I'm sure she'll understand. It's not as if she's totally wild about me."

"But Roger is about me," Chrissy said. "I don't know what I can say to him that won't hurt him."

"Hey—these things happen, Chrissy," Jeff said. "He'll get over it, don't you worry." He looked down at Chrissy's anxious face. "I know how you feel, Chrissy, but you've only got one life, and you've got to do it your way." He lifted his arms dramatically and sang the last few words in an imitation of Frank Sinatra.

Chrissy laughed. "I know, but Roger is so insecure. I'm sure I'm his first girlfriend. I don't know how to let him down gently."

"Well, it's up to you," Jeff said. "But you do want to go out with me, don't you?"

"You know I do," Chrissy said, gazing into his blue eyes. "Don't worry, Jeff. I'll find a way to tell him tonight."

Chapter 17

Chrissy did not see Caroline or Roger until late in the afternoon. The sun had sunk into a broad purple streak off the coast, and the wind had become very cold as they emerged from one of the huts.

Nobody spoke much on the drive home. Chrissy wondered if everyone was just tired, or could Caroline and Roger sense that she and Jeff went off to be alone together? Chrissy sneaked a glance at Roger. *He looks so relaxed*, she thought. *I bet he feels really good about being able to take charge today. Poor Roger. He's so naive, he probably doesn't even suspect that anything could have happened between Jeff and me*, she thought guiltily. *He probably thinks that we went off together to work with the sea lions,*

*just like he and Caroline did. What am I going to
say to him?*

When they reached Caroline's apartment
house, Jeff said, "I don't know about the rest of
you, but I'm exhausted. Holding down five hundred pounds of blubber which is dragging you
into the ocean is really tiring."

"So is bottle-feeding a dozen frightened baby
sea lions," Roger said, climbing out of the car.
"You end up with cod liver oil all over. I'm going
back out there tomorrow. Are the rest of you
coming? I know Caroline said she wanted to."

"That's great, Cara," Jeff remarked. "I guess
you had a good time."

Caroline flushed. "I'm just getting the hang of
it," she said. "I think I can really be useful now."

"I know what you mean. I think I'll go back
tomorrow, too," said Jeff. He didn't even look at
Chrissy, who was pretending to examine a tree
trunk. "I'll call you later, Cara." Then he drove
away.

"And I'll call you later, Chrissy," Roger said. "I
think we'll forget about the movie tonight, if
that's all right with you?"

"Oh, sure, good idea," Chrissy said. Roger
walked off down the hill as Chrissy and Caroline
silently climbed the steps to the apartment.

Do I say something to her now? Chrissy wondered. *Or do I wait for Jeff to call her? Would it
be more fair to warn her that something happened between us? I wish I knew what she's*

thinking. Is she mad at me for leaving her with Roger all day?

The girls reached their room and sat down on opposite beds to take off their wet sneakers.

"So what do you think of sea lions, Cara?" Chrissy asked cautiously, more to break the silence than anything else. "Are they nicer than chickens?"

Caroline's face lit up. "They are fantastic, Chrissy. I see now why you've been so enthusiastic about working with animals at the vet's. I really felt I was doing some good for the first time in my life. I was doing something that wasn't just for me!"

"But you've done lots of things that weren't just for you," Chrissy said. "What about those houses you saved, and the park?"

Caroline looked thoughtful. "They were different because they were for me in a way. If they were destroyed, I wouldn't be able to enjoy looking at them anymore. But this made me feel—almost like God. I thought I'd be no good at it, Chrissy—after making a fool of myself with the chickens and the pigs at your farm—but I was good. I was patient, you see. I kept going until I made the baby sea lions drink the formula."

"Hey, good for you," said Chrissy. "I thought you might be mad at me for leaving you all day with Roger. He didn't bore you too much, did he?"

"Roger?" Caroline asked, and it came out as a squeak. "How could he be boring? He was wonderful, Chrissy. He knows all about sea lions. I learned so much from him."

"Oh, that's good," Chrissy said, crossing one guilty worry off her list.

"And what about you and Jeff? Did you have a good day? Did he keep on fooling around, or was he any use?"

Chrissy hesitated. "Oh, he was fine," she said. "He had a great time grabbing those wild sea lions—you should have seen him, Cara. He wouldn't let go when this huge bull was plunging toward the ocean."

"Oh, that's good," Caroline said.

There was a pause.

"I'm . . . er, sorry we took the picnic," Chrissy said. "We were starving, and we couldn't find you."

"Oh, that's okay. They brought us lunch in the infirmary," Caroline said. "We didn't even bother to come out all day."

"Oh."

Chrissy suddenly felt that the conversation was going nowhere. She obviously couldn't spill the beans until Jeff called Caroline. That wouldn't be fair. She got up. "Do you want the first shower, or do you mind if I take it. I'm all sandy after being dragged along beaches."

Caroline giggled. "That sounds suspicious," she said. "If I hadn't known you were with sea lions all day . . ."

Chrissy's stomach did a flip as she took her robe off the back of the door. "So I'll take a quick shower, then, okay?" *Holy cow,* she thought. *I've got to get out of here before I give something away.*

"Sure. Go ahead," Caroline said, "but maybe I should say something first." The way she looked at Chrissy made Chrissy uneasy. *She knows,* Chrissy thought. *She was just being polite until now.*

"It's about Roger," Caroline went on, playing with the lace-edged pillow on her bed.

"Look, Cara," Chrissy began, "I'd rather not—"

"But I have to tell you right now," she said. "It can't wait, Chrissy. I feel like I'll explode if I don't get everything straight."

"Look, I'm going to talk to Roger later tonight. Won't that be easier?"

"You know what he wanted to say?"

"I've got a good idea."

"And you don't mind—you're not mad?"

"About what?"

"About me and Roger!"

Chrissy tried to focus on her cousin's bent head. "You and Roger?"

"Yes—what did you think I was talking about?" Caroline asked.

Chrissy kept on staring.

"I think he's wonderful, Chrissy," Caroline went one, looking up at her cousin. "The first time I met him, back at the concert, I really wanted to get to know him better."

"You—you did?" Chrissy stammered.

"Oh, sure. He had those dark, serious eyes, and

he knows so much about things. In fact, if he
hadn't been your boyfriend, I'd have gotten to
know him much sooner, but I didn't think that
would be right."

Chrissy shook her head as if her ears might be
playing tricks with her.

"What about him?" she asked. "How does he
feel about you?"

Caroline flushed scarlet. "I think he's fallen for
me in a big way," she said. "The moment we were
alone together, we didn't stop talking once, as if
we'd known each other all our lives." She paused
and looked up at Chrissy. "I hope you're not too
mad at me. I know it's a mean trick to steal my
cousin's boyfriend, but it just happened, honestly."

By now Chrissy had gotten over her initial
surprise and started to laugh. She sat back on the
bed, shaking helplessly with laughter.

"What is it? Chrissy, don't cry. Please, Chrissy,
don't be upset with me," Caroline begged.

"I'm not crying, you dodo—I'm laughing,"
Chrissy gasped.

"I don't get it," Caroline said angrily. "What's so
funny—me and Roger? I don't see anything funny
about that. He's a very nice guy, and I don't know
why you think he's a nerd because I think he's
cute."

"I think he's a very nice guy, Cara," Chrissy
said, wiping her eyes and trying to control her
laughter. "I think you'll both be very happy."

"But?"

"Cara—I was trying to find a way to tell you about me and Jeff," Chrissy managed to say at last.

"You and Jeff?"

"You know I thought he was absolutely gorgeous the first moment I saw him," Chrissy said, calming down now. "Well, today we had so much fun together. And the electricity, Cara—there were sparks everywhere."

Caroline looked at Chrissy and slowly shook her head. "Who would ever have thought it? Do you realize all the time we've wasted, dating the wrong guys?"

"You know," Chrissy said seriously now, "I don't think the time was wasted. Roger would probably never have gotten up the nerve to talk to you if he hadn't been out with me, and I'd never have met Jeff without you, so it all worked out perfectly."

"But what about the prom?" Caroline asked. "We've already bought tickets. I've already talked to Jeff about renting his tux."

"So we switch partners and still go as a foursome," Chrissy said. "We can switch dresses, too, if the tuxes don't match!"

Caroline's eyes glowed. "Won't that be fun? Imagine the four of us all dressed up at the prom. You and Jeff, me and Roger—like a dream come true!"

Here's a sneak preview of *Tug of War*, book number seven in the continuing SUGAR & SPICE series from Ivy Books.

As the girls reached the shore of the lake, they saw a small wooden jetty extending out from a sandy beach area of the camp. A lone figure sat at the end of the jetty, dangling his feet in the water.

Chrissy stopped and grabbed Caroline. "It's him," she whispered. "The cute guy. Take a look at him now and tell me if you think he's gorgeous."

Apparently, the boy had not heard them coming. He stared out across the lake. Caroline took in the sun-streaked hair, the dark tan, the sharp, masculine profile.

"Don't you think he's cute?" Chrissy insisted.

She nodded to Chrissy. "Definitely cute," she whispered.

The boy on the jetty must have heard their voices. He turned around abruptly. Seeing them, he got slowly to his feet.

"Have you been sent to drag me back to camp?" he asked. He gave a little half smile that made him even more gorgeous, revealing perfect white teeth and little laugh lines at the sides of his eyes. He glanced at his watch. "I guess we'd better be getting back." Caroline felt the red creeping into her cheeks under his direct gaze. "By the way," he asked as they began walking, "what's your name?"

Just as Caroline was about to answer, Chrissy opened her mouth.

"I'm Chrissy," she said, "That's my cousin, Caroline."

"I'm Peter. Where are you from?"

"San Francisco," Chrissy and Caroline both said at the same time. Caroline shot Chrissy an evil look and fought back a desire to tell Peter that Chrissy was really from Danbury, Iowa.

"I'm from L.A.," Peter said. "At least, Santa Monica. You know it? Good beaches. Great surf. You guys like surfing?"

"Chrissy does," Caroline said, glancing at her cousin. She could tell that Chrissy remembered her first visit to an ocean, when she had been knocked over by a big wave. Chrissy gave Caroline a warning glare. Caroline grinned, delighted that finally she had been able to score a point.

They reached the camp and paused by Caroline's hut.

"I guess I'll see you guys at orientation in a few minutes," Peter said.

He walked away across the campground. Caroline and Chrissy watched him go.

"What a babe," Chrissy murmered.

"And he seems nice, too," Caroline agreed, staring after him.

"You weren't serious, were you?" Chrissy asked.

"About what?"

"About being interested in him yourself? He really isn't your type."

"I might have decided to change my type."

"Come on, Cara," Chrissy pleaded. "Stop teasing."

"I'm not teasing, Chrissy," Caroline said. She hadn't really planned on becoming interested in anyone this summer, and she was not the type of person, as Chrissy had said, who chased boys. All her relationships with boys so far had happened by accident. She had never, in her life, set out to make a boy notice her and succeed.

Then again, she had never faced the great outdoors before either, and she'd never before been responsible for a group of small human beings. Life was rapidly filling with new experiences. Maybe getting a boy to notice her would be one of them.

"You mean you're really going after this guy?" Chrissy asked in surprise.

"Why not?"

ABOUT THE AUTHOR

Janet Quin-Harkin is the author of more than thirty books for young adults, including the best-selling *Ten-Boy Summer* and *On Our Own*, its sequel series. Ms. Quin-Harkin lives just outside of San Francisco with her husband, three teenage daughters, and one son.